We Never Die

We Never Die

Krishna

ZORBA BOOKS

ZORBA BOOKS

Published by Zorba Books, November 2021

Website: www.zorbabooks.com
Email: info@zorbabooks.com

Author Name & Copyright © Krishna

Title :- We Never Die

Print book ISBN :978-93-90640-38-6
Ebook ISBN :- 978-93-90640-46-1

Zorba Books Pvt. Ltd. (opc)
Sushant Arcade,
Next to Courtyard Marriot,
Sushant Lok 1, Gurgaon – 122009, India

Sri mahaganapathaye namaha

"Drisyam naasteethi bhodena

manaso drisyamarjanam,

Sambannam chedadulpanna

Para nirvana nirvrithi"

'Understand that what all you see are non-existent and so sweep away what all seen and that experience of blankness is the moksha state of mind'.

Vairagyaprakaranam: Sargam1Vairagyolpathyprathipadanam-3. Vasistasudha

Dedicate this book to our family deities.

About the Author

I was born and brought up in Kerala. I am a postgraduate in Geology superannuated from Government service some years ago. Post retirement I function as a consulting Geologist. During my service with the Government and as a consulting Geologist I had the opportunity to travel to many states in India and to countries in the East and West. -I also happened to undertake a long stay in the African continent. My passion to understand the culture and prevailing beliefs in Supernatural realm in different countries has made me interact with people and I am convinced that philosophy anywhere is no different from what I entertained in my life. The progression of science is another weakness of mine.

Acknowledgement

I wish to thank my wife who encouraged me to publish the writing after reading the manuscript. My special thanks to Mr. N. Harikumar, my nephew, and Mr. Rajeswaran Parameswaran, my friend from Africa, for their valuable comments which enabled me to improve the draft. Both of them have authored books to their credit.

I am thankful to the publisher for showing confidence in me, without whom this novella would not have emerged from the manuscript. I am obliged to Zorba Books for guiding me in all the stages. My sincere gratitude to the editors for their patient efforts to make my writing better. I thank all the team members who have worked behind the screen. Without their help this book would not have seen the light of the day.

Author's note

Is it the body or the consciousness that makes the being? What guides our mind and actions, and consequently shapes our character? If all our actions are predetermined, a product of the *'Vasanas'*, how can an individual be responsible for any of their actions? Is there an escape from performing actions? What is Maya or illusion? Is life a simulated reality where the conscious mind may or may not be in the realm of simulation? Is transcending the simulation and merging with the Absolute called enlightenment?

Lately, it appears that human beings are becoming cybernetic organisms. Is it possible what is perceived by our scientists and philosophers as futuristic processes are already in existence in modified forms on distant planets? Is it only a coincidence that several theories propounded by science resemble the observations in the Hindu scriptures or do the finding of the scriptures corroborate scientific evidence?

Science and the scriptures point to the umpteen probabilities of existence of extra-terrestrial beings. Life on earth is suspected to have originated from organic compounds delivered to early earth by meteorites and other celestial objects. The recorded history of the existence of life is just a drop in the ocean of eternity. In such a scenario of several fascinating matters, I decided to write a fantasy novella that centres around a conversation between a fictional character and an alien about the above matters. The novella blends science and belief to peep into the plausible Universal secrets. Subscribing to the Hindu philosophies that life never ends, I have further visualised a screenplay of the past lives of the fictional character concluding that it is through several births and refinement one is able to reach the point where perception will stop because the Absolute generates no holograms.

The plot borrows certain tales and philosophies from the Hindu scriptures and Puranas, and an effort has been made to explore their relation with scientific theories in vogue in the area of computer simulations, robotics, alien interventions and their influence in human history incorporating the hypotheses without prejudice against any of the arguments. In this regard, I have referred extensively to Wikipedia and some of the published articles and copied them, sometimes verbatim, for the sake of building the story acknowledging them in the reference section.

I have referred to the time of happenings in the life of the fictional character, which may not be acceptable to many because the ancientness of the Vedas and epics has always been under dispute pivoting around the composition of the Vedas and migration of Indo Aryans to NW India. It may be noted by the readers that I have not considered the history of the migration of the speakers of the Indo-Aryan language into NW regions of the Indian subcontinent. I lean on the Indian writers and archaeologists who have opposed the notion of a migration of Indo-Aryans into India, and argued for an indigenous origin of the Indo-Aryans which is reflected in the story. I am inclined to subscribe to the observation that the Vedas existed much before the dates ascribed to them since they were orally composed and transmitted without the use of a written script in an unbroken line of transmission from teacher to student. Vedic people never subscribed to writing and Vedas came to cultivate the image of a tradition independent of everything. Consequently, dates attributed by the studies based on composition are sceptical. Ramayana and Mahabharata detail how the protagonists, Rama and Krishna, used Vedic wisdom to engage the society. This means Vedic knowledge was in existence during the time of the Ramayana and Mahabharata.

Similarly there are disagreements with regard to the age of the epics. However, I have relied on the scholars who have given the age of epics based on astronomical information while recounting some scenes in the plot. Dr. Vartak has calculated the date of birth of Rama as December 4th, 7323 BCE and so, the Ramayana occurred 9300 years ago. Mahabharata happened in 3139 BC, and the historical events have been widely documented in Bharathiya scriptures and by great scholars such as Mahakavi Kalidas, poet and literary figure of his time, as well as Aryabhata, the great astronomer and mathematician. The date of the Mahabharata war is 2559 BC according to Nasa.

Similarly, Manusmriti, an ancient legal text or 'Dharmashastra' of Hinduism, describes the social system from the time of the Aryans. In my view, by all accounts, this country is an advanced civilisation that dates back to 3500 BC, even to 6000 or 8000 BC, as observed by some historians.

I had mentioned that Prakrit Sanskrit was spoken in Dholavira village even when no script was available, except for some pictographic representation to convey messages according to the archaeological evidence collected from Dholavira. The images of deities excavated in the Indus valley, as well as the deity in a yoga-like position, suggests that yoga may have been a legacy of the very first great culture that occupied India. In this view, Indian civilization must be viewed as an unbroken tradition that goes back to the earliest period of the Sindhu-Sarasvati (or Indus) tradition (7000 or 8000 BCE).

Preface

Nobody knows how things work in the Universe. On the one hand, when you want something, you often feel that the entire Universe helps you to achieve it. On the other hand, it sometimes feels that the same Universe conspires to give you the taste of failure after failure. I have often felt that several incidents that occurred in my life were repetitions of what had occurred sometime somewhere.

Most of the time I am a good character that matched the definition of the commonly accepted 'good traits'. At times, I have deviated from the so called 'dharma' in spite of the awareness of the ramifications. However, I have had no control over my actions.

In fact, I never believed in astrology or palmistry but when Nadi Josyan started unfolding certain events that had happened in my previous life, I got flabbergasted since most of them mirrored those taking place in the life I endured now. Since that day, my mind has been searching for reasons for every incident that has occurred in my life. I was able to relate these incidents to those said to have happened in the previous life.

This had become a pastime for me whenever I was free from other engagements. I wondered whether I would be able to travel back in time with the help of one of my favourite deities like the characters in Yoga Vasista or become merged with the Universe to a thing of everywhere and nowhere.

Contents

1

Surprise visit from an alien friend

In the wee hours of night, I was woken by a creepy feeling that somebody had broken into the house and was waiting stealthily for something. I broke into a sweat and mustered all my courage to get out of the bed to see what was happening. I peeped into the drawing room but I couldn't see anything except darkness. I groped for the light switch but it felt like it took me a *yuga* to locate it. I gingerly tapped it. The hall glowed with light but I could see nothing except the furniture washed in the light. The eerie feeling that there was someone in the hall still persisted. I reached for the glass mug on the dining table and gulped a mouthful of water to wash down the fear. I was about to return to the bedroom, swearing at my pointless panicking, when I heard a sound. I swirled around to see a tall well-built man standing near the front door.

For a second, I was numb. I could feel the powerful spray of adrenaline and my heart started thudding against my ribs ready to break the cage and escape.

"My dear friend, don't panic," the intruder spoke in a soft voice. He moved closer to me and touched my forehead with his thumb. It was like the touch of a magic wand. The pumped out adrenaline slithered back and I came back to my senses. I regained my composure except for my voice, which wouldn't come from behind the lump that was still choking my throat. The intruder's smooth voice came floating to my ears again.

"My dear, you will be alright. There is no need to worry about me. I am your friend, Partha, and I have come all the way from Planet 'X' to see you and rejoice in your company."

I was awestruck. It seemed so unreal, but his touch on my forehead had stemmed my fear. It had done something to my system and the surged excitement totally disappeared. The lump in my throat also disappeared gradually and I felt completely normal.

"What did you just say? You are my friend and you have come from Planet 'X'?"

I looked at him in astonishment.

"Yes, Kumar. We were close chums in one of our previous lives but I don't live on earth anymore," Partha dropped another surprise on me.

I was wonderstruck to hear my name from his mouth. But the disclosure that he had come from another planet gave me another jolt.

"Kumar, don't rack your brain," Partha continued, "you won't be able to remember or fish out those days from your memory bundle, though it has in store all the lives you lived from the day of your first appearance on this earth or before that. Fortunately, this alien friend of yours can remember all the past lives. It's a gift as a result of being reborn on a Planet where all the beings have the capability to retrieve, project, and see everything stored in their brain."

Was it not similar to the surprise given to Arjuna by Krishna in the *Bhagavad Gita*, when he had told Arjuna that he could remember everything that had happened in the past?

I kept blinking at him. My brain refused to accept that there was someone in front of me who was telling me that he was a friend of mine from the past.

"Won't you offer a chair to your friend and relax?" he inquired with a smile.

"Oh. Sorry. I forgot my manners. Please do take a seat and douse the fire of mysteries ignited by you in me. What do you mean that you don't belong to earth?" His touch had in fact calmed me. It was a calmness I had never before felt in front of a stranger. I was no longer sleepy. I was fully awake and conscious of the situation.

"Kumar," he started again as if to wake me from the trance, "we have lived together along the banks of River Saraswathy when the fragrance of Rama, one of the most worshipped deities on earth, was still in the air. After I was killed in my last life, my astral body travelled billions of miles away from the earth through the interstellar space for some unknown reason. I was born on a planet that belongs to another solar system. On this planet, beings are born with enhanced physical and mental capabilities such as telepathy, telekinesis, time travel, and the capacity to adapt forms as they wish. Our science is several thousand years more advanced than on the earth. In fact, the technological advances made by science on our planet has enabled me to reach you after the elapse of so many years in your time scale."

2

A glance at past lives

Several articles in newspapers, magazines, and umpteen scientific narratives, along with film representations, regarding probable life on different planets that belong to another solar system flashed through my mind. Suppressing my surprise at the very presence of an alien friend, who claimed to have landed from such a faraway planet, I engaged in conversation with him.

"Wow! Should I believe you Partha?" I queried in bewilderment. "So, it is true that extra-terrestrial life exists and there are habitable planets?" I fussed further in an attempt to draw more information from him.

"Your search for extra-terrestrial life mainly focuses on habitability based on earth-like conditions for the emergence of life. You forget that even on your planet, there are creatures who generally live on oxygen, while there are other organisms that prosper without oxygen. There are even some organisms that inhale nitrogen. There is no ideal condition for the existence of life in this vast Universe. Moreover, will you call this body of yours the very life or is it the energy or the consciousness that activates the body that is life? Let us not go to those frontiers because when all the perceptions are seen from a different angle, they will appear to be false. Now, the truth is that we were good friends in our past life," Partha seemed uninclined to elaborate further on that point. Instead, he continued to pull me to the olden days not giving opportunity for me to open an argument.

"I distinctly remember the village on the banks of what you call the mythical "Saraswathy" river where we were born, as well as how joyfully we spent our young days at the Gurukul. I recall the day we were recruited to the army that had been formed by our village heads to stem the attack from the neighbouring kingdom and the insurgencies that erupted within our armed forces during those times. My memory of our weddings is ever fresh in me. The thrill I felt in participating in the family functions and village festivals still gives me delight. Unfortunately, the occasional bouts of fighting between our so-called kingdom and the neighbouring kingdom developed into a terrible war one day. We young captains were destined to fight at the forefront leading our small army of men. We fought valiantly but you were killed during the battle. I was murdered by a rebel from our side a couple of days after the war ended."

Every sentence coming out of his mouth was provoking a reaction and causing an effervescence of unclear and confusing remembrances in me. But I was unable to visualise anything he was talking about.

"Partha, except for the fact that my mind is in a total mess and every cell in me is taut and at the verge of bursting I recall nothing," I blurted out.

"Well. I know the limitations of the human brain and the cells despite their storage capacity. However, as I said earlier the beings from the planet 'X' can project the information stored in their brain like a cinema."

Again, I remembered the words Lord Krishna had said to Arjuna in the *Bhagavad Gita*. He had told Arjuna that he wouldn't be able to remember his past, but Krishna could recall everything that had happened in their previous life.

"Have you heard about mind uploading technology?" Partha sprang a question: the relevance of it jelled in me after a time.

3

Hypothesis in vogue and their existence in an alien world

"Yes, Partha. I believe you're referring to the whole brain simulation, a hypothetical futuristic process of scanning the mental state that comprises the long-term memory and 'self' of a particular brain substrate and copying it to the computer?" I started quoting verbatim what I had learned while researching the subject on Google.

"I'm happy that you keep abreast of the developments in science," Partha said in genuine appreciation.

"Well, my friend. I have read about the probabilities of running a simulation model of the brain's information in a computer such that it would respond in essentially the same way as the original brain and experience a conscious mind," I started revealing my newly acquired information.

Partha acknowledged my familiarity with such matters with a smile and said, "I just mentioned it so that you would be able to understand that what is perceived by your scientists and philosophers already exists in modified forms on distant planets."

"Partha, I am thrilled to hear that these entirely new hypotheses are possible realities on earth and already exist in alien grounds. Yes. Don't you see that human beings are already becoming cybernetic organisms with several artificial organs replacing the original? Similarly, we will perfect the process over time and the newly acquired knowledge will offset many of the present theories. However, I firmly believe that human nature is a Universal state from which human beings emerge and human nature is autonomous, rational, and capable of free will. I am a little worried that the technologies will ruin the fabric of human nature," I added, again quoting from a book I had read some time ago.

"That is a misunderstanding about species that exist on other planets. They too have a free will and are also rational. You might know that the whole universe is tied to a common ethic and aberrations from this collective code of conduct will upset the Universal rhythm. There is an unknown mechanism in nature that will interfere in some form somewhere to regain the balance," Partha elaborated.

4

How Partha Found Kumar

"Partha, the subject is boggling to me. But my present stupefaction concerns how you were able to trace me when you were born thousands of years ago in a different solar system billions of miles away."

"This points to the advancement of science again," Partha almost ignored my statement.

Partha continued his speech, "You see, I told you that we both got killed when the marauders who bothered us frequently attacked us. You were first to fall. I dragged your body some distance away to the premises of an old building and buried you deep for the fear that the barbarian enemies would mutilate your body as part of their victory celebrations. I thought I would recover your body later once the war was over and burn it as per the customs that prevailed amongst us. Unfortunately, the war didn't end as I thought and I was also killed by an arrow a couple of days after you died. As I said I only became aware that my subtle spirit had travelled beyond the interstellar space to another solar system after I became conscious of myself and the planet on which I was born. After some time, I learned to rewind the memory rolls and understood that I earlier belonged to the planet earth which was far away. I made up my mind to visit earth at the first opportunity. When I became the lead on a project that attempted to trace life on other planets, I was happy that my desire could be accomplished one day.

During one of my expeditions to outer space thousands of years ago I landed on earth and on touching the ground I felt a certain familiarity with the land. The innate power in me that makes it possible to scan the recorded past alerted me that I had been here before. The olden times of my life came rushing to my thoughts and I remembered your buried body. The great 'Saraswathy' river had disappeared from the face of the earth and in its place, I could only see a vast expanse of sand. I managed to trace the location by using the kind of laser technology that is in vogue amongst your archaeologists to reconstruct buried treasures. The old structure was spotted deeply buried in the sands of time. I assumed the human form and dug out the remains of your bones and took them to our planet. You may know the advantage of digital storage that explains why chains of nucleic acids have remained the go to biological storage molecule for the past 4 billion years. Your scientists were thrilled to recover DNA molecules that were at least 400, 000 years old from Neanderthal remains, but the recovery of your DNA molecules on a technologically advanced planet that is a few thousand years ahead of the earth was like a simple blood test."

5

Life on Planet X and blend
of our beliefs

"Yes, I understood that part of your explanation. But your statement that 'you assumed the human form' is intriguing for me. Is there no sexual reproduction on your planet? Don't you sport a form like us? Or is it like a simulated reality and you simply appear before me?" I started bombarding him with questions out of excitement.

"Well, that's a lot of questions. Let me explain in two parts. First, let me tell you that we too have a parent body that receives compatible energy or souls that dart out from different planets. It releases the same with capabilities incorporated into it that are suitable for our planet life. You must have also heard of Parthenogenesis, which is a natural form of asexual reproduction in which growth and development of embryos occurs without fertilisation by the sperm."

"Yes, my friend. I have read about such occurrences in invertebrate animal species. I understand it involves the development of an embryo from an unfertilized egg cell and in plants it is a component process of apomixis. I have also read that some species reproduce exclusively by parthenogenesis while others can switch between sexual reproduction and parthenogenesis, i.e., facultative parthenogenesis. But there are no known cases of naturally occurring mammalian parthenogenesis."

"Well... well...on our planet, facultative parthenogenesis is quite common. The Parent body receives compatible energies and we are born with a form as desired by the parent body. We can remain visible or invisible. When we enter other planets, we assume bodies but it is a kind of simulated reality that uses life on that planet as energy sources. For instance, we are like post-human in your futuristic sense where human and technology becomes increasingly involved, a state where we are beyond human beings. You might remember the power of some of the rishis we had encountered along the banks of the 'Saraswathy'. They could assume the bodies of birds or animals at their wish and live incognito."

While Partha was talking, my mind shot to the words of Lord Krishna in the *Bhagavad Gita* when he said to Arjuna, "Partha, you assume this to be my form but it is not. I have assumed a human body by drawing the elements of the earth." The parthenogenesis deliveries on the planet of my friend reminded me of the stories of the birth of Sri Ganesh in Hindu mythology and how Virgin Mary begot a child of her own.

"Our scriptures have many elaborate and extensive references to sex changes and alternate sexual identities."

I started elaborating on my knowledge about the scriptures, which Partha heard without expression allowing me to satisfy myself.

"Although the scriptures never mention homosexuality or bisexuality directly, yet there are tales of Gods or people whose attributes or symbolic behaviour reflects almost the same. They can be interpreted as bisexual or transgender or as having elements of gender variance."

As though reading my mind, Partha said, "There could be aliens who are capable of assuming bodies and living on other planets for long periods, and may be capable of impregnating and producing progenies. However, simulations like mine are possible only for a short period of time. It is unlike the simulated reality where the conscious mind may not be in the realm of simulation. We are both conscious and aware of the surroundings. I just live in a borrowed house; the owner is brain dead but other vitals are intact and he will survive for some more days. I use his body energy to simulate. Nevertheless, we are also bound by Universal law and there is an invisible hand that controls our activities, movements, and our very way of life. This is applicable in case of aliens from any planet or any Solar system."

6

Partha traces Kumar to the Earth

"Partha, it is really interesting to talk with you about science and beliefs. But my knowledge on the subject is very limited and I am sorry to have dragged you away from the subject of the wonderful life we trudged in our previous life. Let us forget about the probabilities and possibilities of our life as holograms for the time being. You are a reality for me now and I am keen to know about ourselves. Coming back to our conversation, how were you able to trace me to this place?"

I just wanted to pick the thread that we had left and suppress the many doubts bubbling in me about the perception of life in the scriptures, as well as recent scientific outlooks about life.

Partha started elaborating without a fuss, "I scanned the people on earth during my second visit in order to find a DNA match of your bone sample. This was not an easy task since the population has increased many fold since I left. I was probably unsuccessful initially because you were in a transition stage between births. However, during the present visit I found a match in the new set of samples. Unknown to you, I scanned your brain and cells to confirm your identity and once I had ensured that you were my old dear friend I dared to appear in front of you."

"Partha, you talk about the transition of birth. Then, what really happened to you after leaving earth?"

"I was born, or rather I became conscious of my presence on planet X, thousands of years ago according to your time scale. I continue to live there."

"Does it mean that one is not conscious during the transition period?" I enquired with curiosity.

"I was consciously unconscious of my transition while the energy or the soul was catapulted to another world. The lapse of time is an enigma. I became conscious of my presence in the new world after the energy, i. e. 'I', was received by a parent body on the other planet and delivered there. I struggled to become acclimated to the surroundings like a new-born. A new life thus started in the new world."

"Is it true, Partha, that we never die? Is it possible that the energy with genetic and acquired characters just escapes the body and later searches or is driven by an unknown force to acquire a new body to fulfil its unfulfilled and cherished desires? Our science has also almost come to the conclusion that this body is not you but you are what the consciousness tells you."

"Are we not part of the Universal consciousness?" Partha retorted with a smile. "Haven't you read in your scriptures that there is no separate individual consciousness but only individual perception and that life creates the Universe rather than the other way around?"

"Yes, Partha. Yogis in ancient India were clearly aware of the universal expanse. They had developed a psycho-somatic-spiritual discipline for achieving union and harmony between our mind, body, and soul, as well as the ultimate union of our individual consciousness with the universal consciousness.

But the problem with the world is that we require empirical evidence in order to believe anything. Science is, however, beginning to acknowledge that our current model of reality is worn out and outdated. It is increasingly pointing towards an infinite universe which our seers had understood a long time ago. It is also acknowledged that what we call space and time are forms of animal sense perception rather than external physical objects. This approach has provided new ways to answer some of the puzzles of mainstream science. Quantum physics confirms that there is no such thing as matter. Everything is light vibrating at specific frequencies. We humans can perceive less than 1 percent of the light and audio spectrum available to us, since 99 per cent of the universe around us is invisible."

"It is interesting to learn the progress scientists on earth have made. But, there is still a long way to go before they are able to clearly understand what had been perceived by the rishis of the past," Partha responded unpretentiously.

"It is to be admitted that science still does not have the ability to explain their theories really," I continued. "However, the latest scientific findings are closer to the truth that life and consciousness are truly fundamental for any real understanding of the universe, which the ancient seers have said undeniably."

He seemed uninclined to delve into the subject further. Perhaps he was hesitant or didn't want to pour universal secrets to an unequipped student like me.

"Partha, you say you are several thousand years old?" I tried to pick the thread again out of inquisitiveness.

"Yes, Kumar. However, you are measuring my age according to your time scale. Our time scale is different."

I remembered the units of time described in the Hindu texts ranging from microseconds to trillions of years, including cycles of cosmic time that repeat general events in Hindu cosmology. Time is described as eternal. Various fragments of time described in the *Vedas, Bhagavata Purana, Vishnu Purana, Mahabharata, Surya siddhanta,* etc., came rushing to my mind. I also ruminated on the calculations of cosmic units of time and the time dilation experienced by different entities. According to the scriptures, time dilation affects the lifespan differently for humans, Pithru (forefathers), Devas (gods), Manus (progenitors of mankind), and Brahma (creator god)."

"I know you are wondering about the longevity of life on our planet, which is pretty long when seen in your time scale."

"Oh, Partha! When you talk about a long life and the DNA tests done on my remains recovered from the desert, I am reminded of a recent article about how aging catches you because of genomic instability caused by DNA damage. If we are able to address the alteration to the epigenome, loss of healthy protein, exhaustion of stem cells etc., we might not age. Maybe you were able to take care of the alterations that cause aging that aided your longevity of life?" I inadvertently poured out my limited knowledge on DNA.

He smiled at me and said "But we do not own a body that rots. We assume a body as per requirements. We draw a different energy from nature to live and our decay happens due to other reasons which I shall speak about later."

"The development on any planet is like drawing wisdom from within or from an unknown source by a brain capable or equipped of it. However, our time also expires like that of any other being in the Universe. The length of our life too depends on tendencies, assumption of bodies, and the activities followed. We are also guided by some code of good conduct akin to that enshrined in your scriptures. Since I remember my life on this planet, I know how constrained we too are by the code of conduct on the planet we live. These are all part of the universal code. Aberrations cause deterioration of power to hold life and we too perish like life here. You gain or lose a credit through your actions, which determines your eligibility for living on that planet. That is the Universal law, my dear," Partha concluded.

His explanation reminded me of the *Aapasthamba Sutra*, which expounded that the gods and humans lived together in the past. As a reward for their sacrifices, the Gods went to heaven but men were left behind. However, humans who performed sacrifices in a manner similar to the Gods would also get a passport to enter heaven. So, Partha might have been a blessed soul that could escalate to a "loka" level above, probably as a reward for his conduct on earth previously. It also reminded me of the characters in the scriptures who tumbled down from heaven to earth because of their uncanny acts, as well as the elation of several virtuous ones from earth to heaven and to other 'lokas' befitting their character.

Other information gathered from science fiction and scriptures through the years flashed through my thoughts. I especially remembered the story of Leela in Vasista Sudha and her travel with her Goddess back in time to trace her husband. If that is true, surely my friend would be able to help me travel. The urge to travel to the past, if not the future, overpowered me to such an extent that my thoughts felt suffocating. I ventured to ask my friend whether there were means for me to re-experience my past life especially the one with him on the banks of Saraswathy.

7

Travel to past lives

Partha said there was no way to travel like Leela as if had read my mind. "I don't have the technology to pick your astral body and carry it with me so that we can time travel. There might be aliens who are probably capable of doing it. But, beware! It would take a lot of time and in return, you will be in a world that is unknown to you. You have lived several lives in the last thousands of years and all the information in you is too much for you to recapitulate and live through."

"Could I at least get a replay of the life I lived in your company?" I pleaded with a sigh of exasperation.

"Oh! Dear, I can see your nerves quivering and the cells trembling, and the brain distended with the desire to travel through time. I shall help you by rewinding the imprints in you by connecting your brain with mine and projecting them on my screen for you," Partha responded kindly.

"Is it similar to the way Sanjayan was able to see the Mahabharatha war?"

"Well, I do know from your history that incidents like the 'Mahabharatha' happened after my disappearance from the earth. I think that must have been similar to a live telecast from the field. You are asking me to rerun your past. The two are different. Now, I intend to project your past on my screen, i. e. akin to computer simulation. I may also get an opportunity to learn the history of the happenings in the span of the last thousands of years in the measure of your time further."

Consequently, he clasped my hand and said, "I shall take you back in time to show you the previous births you have taken one by one and finally, to the days we lived together."

Within seconds, I felt like I was sitting in a high-speed train. The scenes commenced and appeared in front of me with tremendous rapidity. I consciously remembered Leela's journey with her deity in search of her husband, which I had read about in the *Leela Upakyanam* in *Vasishta sudha*; there, she travels in subtle form to the other world. In my case, it is a 'conscious' journey backward while I remained in the same world where I lived.

I wondered and thrilled at the backward journey, enjoying and enduring the days I had lived so far in the descending order. I was running back in age commencing from the recent visit to my daughters and grandchildren in the United States. Then, I started pedalling in between the desert sands of Botswana where modern humans emerged. I was revisiting Kenya, Sudan, Zimbabwe, and South Africa. I became overwhelmed by a sudden sadness when I revisited the death of my mother and father-in-law. I witnessed my retirement from the Government service on superannuation gleefully. I again passed through a deserted feeling on the death of my father. I kept travelling as part of the service, participating and making presentations at several seminars and meetings. I visited many godforsaken places in India as part of my job.

I spent weeks and months in a field related to exploration activities as a young and aged geologist. The days and months spent in France, Australia, Philippines, and Scandinavia flashed on the screen. Time was rushing faster backwards and I remained excited and happy at the birth of my beautiful daughters, my marriage with a wonderful shy, intelligent girl, our lovely relationship, life as bachelor and the exhilaration with friends, the monotonous college, school life, lovely days as a toddler with mum and dad and my struggle to poke into the world while giving pain to my mum, and then sperm and back to nowhere or everywhere…

8

Along the banks of Saraswathy

I got off from my reverie since Partha had taken control. He asked me whether I wanted to continue the journey. I replied that I was curious to witness my earlier lives. However, I requested him to project it starting from our life together to the present like a story in ascending order.

Partha simply smiled and asked me to close my eyes and held my hand again for a few seconds. Again, I slipped into a trance and felt like I was thrown into an entirely new world.

I found myself on the banks of the mighty Saraswathy, flowing with all its glory. The drama of my life started unfolding in a rather slow motion. I was born not exactly on the bank of Saraswathy but in Dholavira village on the bank of "Nadar", one of its tributaries. A cluster of villages dotted the landscape, east of the river, with neatly thatched independent houses made of red bricks. A graded pathway ran across the village to enable the movement of men and livestock. The clusters of villages together formed our small kingdom, although such a concept was not prevalent in those times. There were no clear-cut boundaries. The river was the boundary to the west and the Thar desert to the east. Rapids in the far north formed the northern boundary and the border to the south was where the villagers did not go. The so-called kingdom was hardly 10 sq. km. We never had a king or priestly king to rule the tiny land. The villages were run by a council of wise old men who were respected by the villagers. In fact, they ruled the villages through the implementation of some unwritten laws that were more akin to *Sanatana dharma* without any connotation to religion, class, or creed. We believed only in following a way of life designed to ensure peace and tranquillity, and the sustenance of life without mental or physical agonies. Everybody did every kind of job according to their interest, but it was ensured that there was no dearth of men in the area of requirement. The children were trained in all disciplines ranging from farming, masonry, carpentry, art, architecture, and martial arts, a legacy left by Parasurama. Our elders referred to Parasurama as a fighter and teacher.

We had no Gods or temples unlike what we have heard of the west where the religious system blended political with spiritual elements. We have heard about how their city states were ruled by patron gods and goddesses and how the priestly class had spoiled the social fabric and societies. Our elders were scared to incorporate Gods and Goddesses into our system and give way for a priestly class who would in turn, take over the administration in the name of the God and divide the people. However, Nature was the only God for us. The way of our simple living was the religion with no name or whatsoever. Veda was taught by intellectuals to impress the grandeur of 'Brahmam' and to detail the interconnection of everything in nature and the resultant outcomes through such networks. Relative weight was given to the recited version of the Veda. In this manner, we memorised the knowledge and everything functioned smoothly. We spoke Prakrit Sanskrit but had no well-founded script, except for recording the trading in some form of pictographs.

We did not have a standing army to defend our unmarked boundaries when I was young. However, I saw a few youngsters being trained in weaponry and martial arts. They were assigned to protect the villages from wild animals and marauders from beyond the forest who looked for opportunities to steal food grains and livestock. There was a bond among us and we shared everything from food to emotions and lived peacefully.

Beautiful farms spread to the west of the villages for several *kosa*, and were close to the flood plains of the active stream. Water was plentiful because of the perennial river and so, the crops were plentiful and our granaries were overflowing most of the year. Further, to the east of the villages the ground opened to green fields with grass and shrubs for a good distance and then raised and rolled on to small mounds. Green fields provided grazing ground for the cattle and sheep, another wealth of the village. Beyond the small mounds lay the mango groves that merged with the forest. The forest ended at the edge of the Thar desert. Marauders made occasional visits to the villages from beyond the forest and spoiled our crops. They also looted food grains, sheep, or cattle sometimes. The villagers took arms only in defence and the looters who were caught would be warned and sent back to the forest most of the time. Some of them were inclined to stay back and help us on the farms. They would accept grains, fish, and meat in return for their service. Later, they started coming in bunches seeking work and the elders gracefully offered them odd jobs. They spoke a different tongue and had features different from us. In spite of our best efforts to absorb them into our fold, they wanted to stay independent and started forming colonies close to the forest. This was a matter of concern and the elders sometimes considered whether it was an unwise decision to have permitted them entry and equally, was it imprudent to let them build colonies of their own? We had heard of the demographic genocide and culture annihilations from such infiltrations in the long run. But we hesitated to act out of compassion and consideration for the women and children and the matter gently started slipping from our hands. The major factor that influenced our decision to leave the migrants alone was because of their love for drinks and unholy practices. Incidences of bouts among them were common and we suspected that they would spoil our youngsters. However, our elders believed in tolerance and thought time would heal the injuries if there were any altercations. They used to say that we were also migrants from the far south. Otherwise, how did we hinge and share *Manusmrithi* and how did our art and architecture bear resemblance to those in the south? However, we did not follow 'Manumrithi' in toto. We took only the cream and implemented it here and there in order to ensure social order based on liberty, equality, and fraternity as contemplated therein. Time rolled and instead of peace the days churned out more complications. Our marshals were frequently compelled to barge into the territories of the new colonies to catch the troublemakers and isolate them in fenced quarters. Slowly, the non-violent ways of living of the villagers were getting marred by these people, the heavy price for the benevolence shown.

We had surplus food and cattle and so, we traded them with people in the east and west for fine clothes and jewellery. The elders cautiously approved certain imports and controlled the avariciousness that spiked among some of the traders to make more profits. Amassing wealth and materials was discouraged in the society because it would create distinction among the villagers. The elders feared that this would threaten the egalitarianism that was preached and practiced in the villages, which would lead to elitism and ruin the social fabric.

I was born in one of the villages in Dholavira and my friend, Partha, belonged to a neighbouring village. We formed a good company tending the cattle, grazing them and putting them back in the barn. We were sent to study farming, fishing, art, architecture, and engineering technologies under the experts in the field when we came of age. We were also taught martial arts so that we would be able to defend ourselves and the villagers. The training went on for 15 regnal years. The elders kept me as a reserved soldier for emergent situations since I was good in weaponry and martial arts. Otherwise, I was engaged in construction and farming.

Partha was extremely good in all technologies. He was blessed with an excellent brain and he absorbed knowledge like a sponge. He had a good heart and helped the needy, but when required he could be a terror to the villains.

He was so skilful that when he observed the vagaries of the monsoons, he suggested ways of combatting the impending water shortages to the council of advisers. He also advised them to construct check dams and spillways across rivers to augment water. He helped the engineers to prepare blueprints for the same. His skills in fishing and farming were talked about in the village. He was my hero and I followed him like a shadow.

Partha and I cultivated a bond despite our interests and approach to matters. He never missed to include me in any of his initiatives. He had a 'character' that was lacking in me because of my unsteady mind. He firmly believed in what the elders preached and practiced, though he questioned them every now and then on different issues. But his questions were always well thought out because he wanted to clarify matters for himself, unlike me who was critical of things without any depth in the subject. I lingered unnecessarily on issues and my aberrations from the ethos worried Partha. He used to advise me to view matters with the right perspective and in the larger interest of the people. Though my mind wavered I tailed him everywhere and supported the cause like a disciplined soldier. Partha had a very good heart and helped the needy disregarding his health and wealth. He had an aura about him and a sway over the public. The villagers saw their future in him. One day, his name was suggested to the council of the decision-making body and the elders accepted his inclusion wholeheartedly. He was in the forefront of every project as labourer, engineer, and administrator. He used to organise a crop festival every season, which was celebrated by the villagers with great pomp and show. People would be invited from neighbouring and distant places and our finely crafted potteries, bangles, and tools would be displayed for everyone. We used a lot of copper and bronze to make vessels and figurines, as well as weaponries for soldiers.

I used to tell everything to my wife, a village woman of deep and restrained character. Though rustic, she was fundamentally detached from attachment to the material world. She was my wife but she never approved of my restive character and hated my fluctuating interest in art, music, martial arts, along with my flight in imaginative worlds.

"Why don't you stick to one matter at a time? Why do you dwell in imaginations that only give you worries?" It is absolutely true that I spent a lot of time deliberately and inadvertently blowing several trivial matters to disproportionate sizes to a point of rupture that does not even merit casual attention. I continued to waste precious hours imagining for the sake of pleasing myself or wildly visualizing scenarios that had not yet occurred, quelling the seething bitterness in me for something unknown. Was it jealousy or inquisitiveness that troubled me? Or did I aspire to rule the land? I lived with hundreds of desires in spite of my knowledge of the *Vedas* and *Upanishads* and awareness about the futility of acquiring material possessions.

"You have resolved a hundred times not to take anything emotionally," my wife would rebuke me whenever I reacted to matters that were insignificant and could have been ignored. "Have your philosophies vaporised at the altar of burning desires? I fear that instead of maturing and seasoning, your mind is becoming fickler. Only more miserable and wasteful days lie ahead if you continue in this manner," she kept chiding me. Her words neither ignited any anger in me nor doused the cravings that were scorching me because I knew them to be true.

But the very nature of my mind was receptive to all calamities and my reactions were impulsive. I wondered if I would escape from this nature of mine? Partha was also aware of my nature but he never left me alone and always tried to steer me in the correct direction. My dependability on him also increased because of my confused mind. The elders did not approve of me for certain jobs but believed in Partha's ability to control my zealousness.

Seasons folded and time moved swiftly onward.

We were past middle age when the rare squabbles with regard to import and exports with the neighbouring kingdoms aggravated to occasional fights. The failure of crops in the neighbouring kingdoms meant they wanted more help from us. But our council decided to keep the grain reserves as we too were under threat of water shortage at times. We were compelled to form a permanent army much against our wishes to guard our granaries and borders. Problems were brewing within the community of looters turned helpers. The youngsters in their community who were unaware about their own history of migration, a gracious offering of our people, refused to heed their elders' advice. The colonies needed to be frequently policed in order to quell rebellions. There were several youngsters from the colonies who had been recruited to our army, and they would often be instigated to mutiny by the neighbours. We were forced to oust them from service and consequently, they formed a rebel group.

The youngsters in our villages wanted to dismantle the colonies and drive them to the Thar desert. It had become a herculean task to control our own youngsters in spite of the promises they had given to the council not to take arms for anything and everything. Peaceful days were bidding farewell and the general happiness that prevailed in our tiny kingdom was replaced by anxiousness. Partha and I never had rest. We were always on the run trying to solve the problems mushrooming in different quarters. Partha was against uprooting the migrants and imposing capital punishment on rebels. He was of the opinion that we should not create heroes from amongst the protesters. He was one of the senior counsellors now and was revered by many. Nobody wanted to displease him though they had reservations about his decisions. I worked as his sidekick. The village life had changed considerably within the last few decades. We wondered whether the 'Varnasramas' and class creed distinctions that had been established in the other kingdoms were a solution to control the situation and whether the god men and the intertwining of politics and religion was a way out to keep the unruly people at bay.

Years passed and an open war started between the neighbouring territories. Partha and I led the soldiers to the western border where the serious insurgencies were happening. I remember getting stabbed in the back and before losing consciousness saw my friend rushing to my rescue.

9

Failed King and his traumatic spiritualism

I was born to a benevolent ruler of a small country. After taking reign from father, I was mostly engaged in the pursuit of music and arts with no time for administration. I refused to listen to the advice offered to me from the benefactors. The borders of the country remained insecure. They were infested with enemies who were looking for opportunities to snatch power from me. I lived a peaceful life but the people lived in fear and anxiety. They wished somebody would replace me. Their wish was fulfilled one day by a king from the neighbourhood. He simply swept in with a few soldiers as if he had come for a party and took over the reins from me. I was banished to the forest to continue singing and dancing in the wilderness. In this *janma* as well, my queen was a quiet and graceful lady who remained unperturbed even in the midst of a crisis. We both managed to escape to the bank of the Sarayu River and I planned to commence a spiritual life to attain 'the knowledge' and remain a saint. I thought it was an easy job like walking to a shop to buy groceries.

I went to a Guru to learn about the Brahmam. I had some basic knowledge of Vedas and Sruthi, which had been taught to us when we had been in the *gurukul*. We had also been taught the art of sword fighting, archery, fist fight, etc. But the philosophies that had been taught to me to gain control over one's mind had not jelled in me because my concentration had always been somewhere else. My studies had been mechanical and the mental balance intended to be achieved by such studies remained distant.

Before admitting me, the Guru asked me about my identity which I told him without reservation while gloating in the past. The Guru heard me out and advised me to forget the past first, learn to calm my mind, and stay in-pulsated by activities around me and then come to him. I meditated for long hours and survived on frugal food. My mind was still in turmoil. However, I went to seek the Guru's feet after a year and prostrated before him. He was reluctant to recognise me and asked who I was. I was astonished and told the Guru, "I am the king…" before I was able to complete the sentence, he roared, "You are still living in your past glory," and closed the door of the *matha* on my face.

This time I understood the essence of the Guru's statement but I still did not know how to delete the history in me. My kingdom and its subjects were still in my mind and the mistakes I had made were gnawing at me. I returned to my wife and shared what had happened with her. She told me very blatantly that I was not qualified to enter the field of *sanyasam* and I couldn't become a *kjani* unless I changed my mental attitude.

"The prerequisite for Sanyasam is the mental strength to develop a detachment towards everything. You are unable to develop detachment because you still love your country and people, and are smarting from the guilt of not doing justice to the people as a king," she observed. She said the best option was to return to our country and try to take over the reins of the kingdom by driving the enemies out instead of loitering around the forest achieving nothing. Once I had gained control over my kingdom, I could focus on calming my mind. After fulfilling my duties as a king, I could entrust the land to secure hands and then seek Vanaprastha.

"You will start realizing that the 'knowledge' that you are seeking is not anywhere outside but well within you," she tried to open my eyes and continued to say that my subjects or advisors never hated me but my sloppy and irresponsible attitude in the midst of crisis had infuriated them. My attitude had been the sole reason they had wished for my being ousted. "Everybody knew you were a good fighter and you could have led your army to success. But you left some chieftains to defend the land and continued to indulge in your blasted interests. You still have time to knock the enemy down and take the reigns back before he establishes himself well," she sermonised for a while and then fell silent so I could reflect on what she had said.

I brooded over what she said for a week. Yes. I had not fulfilled the promise given to the people during the coronation and the present sufferings of the people were because of my laxity. I had accepted the banishment and tried to run away from my responsibilities and escape in Vedanta.

I learned that the Commander and the Generals controlling the kingdom on behalf of their King were taking it easy because I had not attempted any adventures in the last year. Their spies had informed them of my meeting with a Guru to enter the field of *Sanyasa*. It was the best opportunity; my Commanders opined to attack and win back the sovereign.

Over the next year, I tried to stay within the borders of my country discreetly. I contacted my old guards and ministers who had also escaped into the woods. We slowly started collecting men and materials through villagers who still respected their old King. Our army expanded but we gathered in different places ready to assemble at a common place when it was time for the attack to commence. We attacked the palace during the peak of winter, searing through them. The palace was captured easily since we gave no time to the Commander and Generals to access help from any quarter. They were arrested and the borders were closed by seasoned fighters on our side. The war barely lasted a week. I took the bridles back in my hand and for the next couple of years I worked with the people to reconstruct everything that was in shambles. Within a decade, we had regained our past glory and the peace and prosperity that had prevailed in the kingdom during the period of my forefathers. The much sought after quietness in mind that the Guru talked about started descending on me. All the while, my wife had been aloof. She remained in her thought world. She never interfered in the administration. If I asked her for her opinion, she would give a few practical suggestions and tell me to test the advice before implementing it.

Time flew by. One day, I left the kingdom with my wife with a clear mind and moved to the banks of Sarayu wondering whether I would be able to meet the same Guru who had previously turned me down. Luckily, I found him. He opened the door for me with a smile and said I was ripe enough to be his disciple. He advised me to learn everything on my own and only visit him when I wanted to clarify any doubts, like Varuna running to Brahma in the *Taittiriya Upanishad*. We both aged and our pursuit to acquire 'the knowledge' often told in the *Upanishads* continued until our body ceased to function.

10

The Explorer and his tragic end

The scenes kept changing. Suddenly, I was a worker searching for gold and copper in the mountain range of Aravalli. We, the workers, were settled in a remote village tucked between two hillocks in the Aravalli range somewhere NE of Avandi and SW of the Matsya kingdom. I had taken up the job, the legacy left to me by my great grandparents to my father who had passed it on to me. There is nothing spectacular about young age. I grew up with boys and girls of the same age playing, fighting, and helping my parents in many ways. Vishnu and Siva bhakti were instilled in us through stories told to us by our grandparents and the folklore common among the people in the villages concreted the belief. Rama and Krishna were quoted for anything and everything and they were our Gods, heroes and epitome of everything. We would be told the stories of the Great War that had occurred a few generations ago somewhere in the north east in great detail as if the elders had witnessed it themselves. It was said that a few men from the village had in fact joined the army that marched from Avandi and Chedi to participate in the war. They said *kanayya* had passed through our village on his way to Dwaraka and our soil was blessed with his footprints. Duryodhana and Karna had also come to our village during their search to find the Pandavas who had been living incognito in the Matsya kingdom. Although these men were villains in the stories that we had been told, the old men in the village had a thousand tongues to praise both those who had passed through the village and mingled with the villagers, as well as others who had presented a few of the villagers with gold, pearls, etc. I had in my possession a ring that had supposedly been presented to my great great grandfather by Karna many generations ago. I kept it as a treasure.

Well. My job was to trace the gold lode indications in rock where a team of people would dig and collect the rock pieces with gold incidences. I had another group of people who would pound the rock pieces in pits dug in the outcrops and the powder would be winnowed to collect the heavy gold. We sold great quantities of the gold that was collected to a trader in the town through a goldsmith in the village. Additionally, we used to wash the fines collected after winnowing, which we used to take to the rivers and pan to win the remaining gold. These small collections could also be sold to goldsmiths who would pay us extra for them, and the profit would be divided among us. The trader used to provide tools for our work and also pay us grains, clothing, and copper coins for buying other necessary essentials. This was our life and there was no intervention from the king's men or any avaricious merchants except for some thugs who waylaid our men to snatch the gold collections. The village heads had a posse of armed men who used to protect us from attacks by burglars. There were several workings for gold in the Aravalli range and gold was in plenty. The gold generally went to the coffers of the chieftains and ultimately, the bounty reached the treasury of the Matsya, Avanti, Chedi, and Sourashtra kings who controlled Dwaraka, which was the prime trade centre before the deluge. Our forefathers had heard of the great flood that devoured Dwaraka and the temple constructed by Vajranabha where the residential palace of his great grandfather, the Lord Krishna, had earlier been located. It was considered a sacred place and a few of the villagers had made journeys to Dwaraka.

Though the floods had left no mark of the old beautiful city, the merchants who made frequent visits to Dwaraka told us about the endeavours made by the present rulers to recapture the pride of the olden times, by establishing fresh trade routes and opening several warehouses for storing the goods for import and export.

We never bothered about how the gold was traded after it left our hands because we were happy that we never had to suffer a dearth of food or clothing, and we also had nice thatched houses in which we lived. A perennial river flowed through the village and the village head took care of our secure living. We were a happy lot since our needs were limited and because we had not seen the opulence of the towns that were far away or mingled with people of affluence and our minds had not yet been corrupted. We had our fun, family, and friends. Images of Rama, Krishna, and Siva were venerated in small temples that had been constructed based on the hearsay style of the temples in the big towns from the merchants.

Time was running out and I got married to a very god fearing and beautiful girl. My wife was excellent at nursing and very shrewd in finding suitable herbs for making pastes and soups for different diseases and injuries. She was indeed a tireless and selfless worker who was loved by the people in the village. Thirty years passed and our children migrated to the town seeking a job to get away from the dreary and limited jobs in the village, and settled there. We had visited them but the town life did not suit us and we soon returned to our village. We were getting old and thought it was time we retired and pursued our long-cherished dream of visiting Dwaraka and Somnath. I talked to the village head of our desire and he introduced me to some merchants who made regular visits to Dwaraka to sell and buy merchandise. Several carts passed through our village and we got onto one of the carts that was going to Dwaraka with goods and travelled with them. The carts were well-equipped with food and water, and a band of security guards walked along to thwart any challenge posed by bandits en route. It took over 15 days for us to reach Dwaraka and we settled in one of the travel houses recommended by the trader for pursuing our goal. Such houses were run by rich merchants and the accommodation and food were free for the pilgrims who often came to Dwarka from faraway places.

We dipped in the River Gomathy, entered the temple, and prostrated before the Lord. We felt like we didn't want to ever leave the temple. We went to Dwarka when the Krishna Janmashtami festival was taking place, and the place was thronged with sadhus, swamis, and saints from different kingdoms. During Janmashtami, the devotees would fast for 24 hours, offer milk sweets to the baby Krishna, and light wicks soaked in *ghee* (clarified butter) during the midnight *arati*. We participated in all the rituals happily. I had not seen my wife so happy in her entire life and I was doubly happy that I could accomplish it for her. Discourses on *Kanayya* were regular in the temple and songs on the Lord by devotees filled the air. We befriended a few devotees who suggested we visit the Rukmani temple and Bhalka 'theertha' from where Lord Krishna ascended to Vaikundha. The way to both places was tough with wild shrubs and narrow paths. Both of us were very sad and cried profusely when we heard about how the Lord was killed by Jara's misfired arrow because he had mistaken the lord's feet for a deer's ear. More than this it was heart-breaking to hear about the Lord's disappointment about the Yadavas fighting amongst themselves on the beaches of Dwaraka, and how Krishna went to Bhalka theertha to meditate under the banyan tree. We heard the story of why Rukmani had a separate temple when the main deity and others remained in the Dwaraka temple. We spent about six months in Dwaraka and also did some odd jobs in one of the warehouses to make some money along with visiting the temples. We were lucky to join a group who made their way to Somnath and with the Lord's blessings had good dharsan. We stayed there with the group for a month and returned to Dwaraka.

We were thinking of returning to our village when we heard the sadhus, Brahmins, and others talking about Badrinath. Their intention was to start the journey at the beginning of spring and reach Badrinath by mid-autumn. My wife expressed her desire to accompany them but we had no idea where Badrinath was located and the distance we had to tread. However, we expressed the same to one of the sadhus who pouted his lips for some time and finally asked us to tail them during the journey.

The sadhus used to trek the path that was supposed to have been taken by Lord Krishna to reach Mathura and from there God willing, we would've been able to reach Badrinath before the harsh winter set in. My wife held my hand in excitement at the thought of Mathura and Vrindavan. Her eyes reflected her deep desire to visit the holy sites. But I was hesitatant about how this small, tender woman would be able to walk all the distance. The journey to Dwaraka from our village and to Somnath had all been in bullock carts and her soft feet never suffered the hard and rough paths. Already she had thinned and darkened in the hot blazing summer of Dwaraka. However, her determination won and we joined the group of people who were led by the sadhus so that we could get the blessings of Krishna in Mathura and Vishnu of Badrinath.

We kept chanting slokas, singing songs in praise of the Lord, and stayed in villages on the way where sadhus were respected and food provided. The journey continued for about three months. We reached Mathura when it was autumn. The devotees were respected by the people all along and my wife's dream was fulfilled when we saw the Lord in the temple and walked the gardens in Vrindavan where Gopis were blessed by Krishna.

Time rolled. It was to satisfy my wife's desire that I made enquiries with pandits, Brahmins, and sadhus about Badrinath and how I could accomplish the wish of my better half. I would not have ventured the trip had I got wind of the future. Autumn was folding and winter was at the threshold when some Brahmins from Mathura decided to travel to Badrinath. We went to them, prostrated in front of them, and voiced our desire to follow them admitting that we had no idea where Badrinath was or which route was to be taken. They took pity on us and allowed us to join their retinue which contained musicians, dancers, and a caravan with food. We also joined the bandwagon as helpers and commenced our longest journey. It was when winter had just set in that we reached Haridwar and trekked to Rishikesh and finally to Badrinath. The travel and hard work had taken a toll on my wife's health and while we were in Badrinath she fell unwell. Before the local *chikilsak* could do something she simply passed away leaving me in a lurch. I had no money to cremate the body. Finally, I sold the ring of 'Karna', which had been given to my forefather, to a merchant who didn't even bother to hear the story about how I had acquired it or its worth but fixed a price that I had to accept. I had no bargaining power in the unknown place and collected the essentials with the money he offered to perform her last rites. I was practically shattered after her departure. I cried bitterly to the Lord, why 'He' has taken her away so prematurely. Is this the *punya* I had gathered by the *dharsana*? I cursed the gods for snatching my life's treasure from me. The philosophies I heard all this time about *jeevatma* and *paramatma* vaporized in the agony of loss. When Lord Siva, the quintessence of "knowledge", went mad with grief and shook the earth with *Thandava* carrying his wife's charred body, how come this poor villager could restrain his sorrow and act sane. It did not strike me in the overwhelming loss that this could possibly have happened even when we had been in our village. I kept roaming the paths of Badrinath like a mad man yelling and crying bereft of food or clothing. People mistook me for a mad sadhu. Finally, I succumbed to hunger, thirst, and biting cold in the peak of the winter.

11

An animal's life

Time rushes forward further and in the succeeding life I see myself as a lion in a forest somewhere in north India. Is it the Gir forest? I am the fourth puppy to my parents. But unlike my siblings who always snuggled between the legs of our mother, I had an exploratory nature and wandered in the bushes ignoring the warnings of my parents. Our habitat was in a corner of dry scrub land and open deciduous forest a little away from one of the perennial rivers. One day, when my family was resting under a tree after a sumptuous meal of deer meat hunted by my father, I slipped away into the forest looking here and there with bulbous eyes taking in the beauty of the forest. I do not know how long I strolled. Suddenly, I became aware of the burning eyes of golden hyenas not far away from me. I ran into a pit under a giant teak tree and hid. After some time, I could hear the roar of my dad driving the hyenas away but I dared not to come outside for fear of reprimand. I must have slept off because it was getting dark when I poked my head out of the pit. Ensuring there was no threat of hyenas; I started running towards my family but I could not see them anywhere. My parents had probably thought that I had fallen victim to the hyenas who had moved in large numbers to this side of the forest and considering the safety of my siblings, they must've moved to some other place. I did not know what to do and ran hither and thither with disappointment. Finally, I returned to the river bank. Suddenly, I heard the giggling of the hyenas and jumped into the river out of fear. I swam desperately with no idea where I was going, but I managed to reach the other bank. I continued running deep into the unknown area. I climbed onto a maple tree and found a safe place. At that time of year, this part of the forest was temporarily infested with Sambar, Chingara, Cheetal and I moved with them for some time. They didn't run away from the harmless toddler. I fished from the river at times, batting the fish with the palm, a trick my dad had taught me sometime ago. I kept regretting my impudence but soon gained confidence and was able to look after myself and learn the jungle laws. Several seasons came and went and I grew in size with time. I kept drifting carefully to other territories and ended up with a group of lions and lionesses who suspected my appearance and challenged me. But my size and ferocious nature made them accept me. However, my mind was looking for something and I never knew what it was. Into such a lonely life came a lioness who accidentally sauntered into my territory while chasing a Cheetal. We soon became partners. Now, I have a family and puppies. However, my mind was not at rest. My queen also seemed to be lost in thoughts most of the time. The excitement I had when I had been younger seemed drained out of me and I despised the quiet life that mostly included resting under some tree with an occasional run behind some prey when my queen and puppies cried of hunger. I used to think how happy the Sambar, Cheetal, Chingara and other animals were who never hurt anybody. They seemed always engaged in grazing the grass or nibbling the leaves of the tree and sprinting around. There were a number of reptiles moving about who never bothered anybody, only the crocodiles in the rivers were a bit ferocious and dangerous. They mostly confined themselves to the banks of the river and seldom crept into the forest. I felt all the life around including the trees and plants that wafted in the wind and bloomed during different seasons were happy and I never knew the real meaning of happiness. Though I roared and scared the beings around, I pitied myself about my mundane routine with no exhilaration except during the fight for survival.

I had always hunted with disdain and pitied the animal who was in my grip. There were times I had let the animal escape and returned with hunger to the amazement of my queen who then would go out for the kill.

When I rested, which was what I did most of the time, I tried hard to think beyond the point of hunger. I wanted to know what the other animals thought. When I was not able to comprehend the feelings of my queen, how on earth could I learn the thoughts of beings around me? I had seen the two-legged species poaching the animals and they communicated with each other with jeers, wave of their hand, etc. Like other animals, I also never dared to confront them because they were cunning. They never fought with their hands or legs but used weapons to attack us.

I loathed my life and all the frustration gushed out as a growl or roar that scared the poor animals in the forest. My queen, who always remained discreet, walked out of my life one day just as my kids had done. I am alone now with my thoughts. This never escalated beyond a certain level, though I crammed my brain to understand the world around me more. The real problem was that I did not know what I really wanted. I had often observed that when I chased a Sambar, Chingara, or any other animal one of them stayed back and let itself be caught to save the others. The animal could have made me pursue it for much longer but either out of pity for me or concern for its herd, it paused deliberately and offered its body to me. When I pounced on it, it gave a wan smile that used to send a chill in my heart. I could not understand my feelings? Did my other friends also feel similarly? I was getting fed up with seeing the agony of my prey but this blasted hunger would never let me stay put and it almost drove me nuts. What was the way out?

My introspection continued. When the animals went limp on my grip what happened to them? After I ate their body where was it then? Suppose I fell victim to some other animal or to those two-legged species, what would then happen to this 'I'?

"Am I free when the body is lost?" I was lazing one day on the banks of a swollen river flowing bank to bank with eddies here and there. I saw the lifeless bodies of several animals floating in water. Had the river become ferocious to liberate the beings from their agonies? Somebody seemed to be telling me from within that the lifeless situation could be the end to the misery and road to freedom. I mused for some time and in a frenzy, I simply jumped into the river and the current swiftly took me a long distance. I didn't try to swim or come out of the water. I allowed the water to devour me and lost consciousness.

Was it a kind of suicide?

Hunger and desire are the two things that dictate our life. Memories of Pakkanar, the saint from Kerala came to my consciousness while the reel of my past life was still running. One day, Pakkanar felt very hungry but had no money to buy food. He saw a cart loaded with fruits. The vendor was not nearby. He fought over whether to help himself with some fruits or not. His hunger won the senses and he pinched two bananas from the cart. Pakkanar was caught red-handed and the crowd duly punished him by thrashing him without mercy. Pakkanar did not resist but asked the crowd to beat him further, crying aloud that it was 'He' who did not listen to 'Him' and deserved severe punishment. Who is this He? It was the body he meant by 'He'. Pakkanar considered his body to be a separate identity from him because this body is not you but only a perishable carrier and *anityam*. But *nithyam* would never perish.

I was then a poor animal who was unable to comprehend the identities of the body and the true 'I'. However, something gnawed at my senses and my thoughts jumped past the limitations of the animal brain. Finally, though I was unable to completely understand the matters, it became apparent to me that the body was only the carrier of "I" and wanted to escape from the cage. This feeling from within drove me to Jalasamadhi.

12

Life of a vagrant merchant

The next thing I saw was that I was a successful merchant somewhere in Madurai. I had been born to a wealthy merchant. I had had a good education and was also taught the nuances of the trade. I travelled a lot with my father to the neighbouring kingdoms, which were then mostly controlled by Rajathi Raja, the Chola Emperor whose kingdom had extensions in Sinhala, Java, Sumatra, Indonesia, and Vietnam. I chanced to travel to those countries pursuing and expanding my father's business. However, I lived the life of a vagabond for the most part of my youth. Once I returned from the business tour, my parents decided to put an end to my wayward life. I was married off to the only child of another rich merchant. Though I knew it would put an end to my loose life, I agreed because despite all my exciting adventures, I was feeling empty and that was disturbing my consciousness.

The girl I married was quite young and petite, but behaved more mature to her age. She rarely showed the emotions expected of a teenager. I loved her very much but kept drifting quite a lot to fill the emptiness in my heart, which kept increasing by the day. It engulfed my thoughts and mind and transformed me into a kind of zombie.

At the time, Madurai was under the control of the Cholas, but the people were still fond of their Pandya king who had escaped to Simhala, their ally, with his Chera wife. Pandya was trying to break the iron clad and recapture Madurai and a lot of skirmishes were happening here and there. But the Cholas were too strong for them to make a dent. Rajaraja the emperor was a follower of Shaivism. However, he was tolerant towards other faiths and supported the construction of several temples for Vishnu and even encouraged the construction of the Buddhist Chudamani Vihara. However, Buddhism was in the waning stage like Jainism. Buddism was also wafting to the shores of Simhala, Java, and Sumatra to the east.

Under such circumstances, I had a lot of opportunities to visit Saivite and Vaishnavite *mathas*, as well as Buddha Viharas where I searched for a fountain to fill the void in my heart. I travelled as part of the business to several countries, and often met several monks and sanyasis from whom I was able to learn the very knowledge that was lacking in me. It was during those times Rajaraja built the Brihadishwara Temple. My father also contributed towards the construction with men and money. I fell at the feet of Brihadiswara to teach me a way to quench my parched heart.

But the feelings of emptiness persisted as before. My life partner, a very calm and collected woman, allowed me to continue the search without any interference or comment. I felt a little odd and wondered whether she cared for me at all. But one day when I was drifting in my thoughts, she queried whether I had been successful in my search for tranquillity. I said "No" very disappointingly. She remarked that I was trying to fill the void by engaging with people who also had a void in them and so, I would never be able to fill it. Her comment suddenly hit me hard and paralysed my thoughts. First, I had not been expecting such a comment from a source who appeared to me as lacking philosophical inclinations. She continued her speech "What have you achieved in all these years except tormenting your mind and body searching for a thing that does not exist outside? Don't you find life just an illusion my dear, or just a 'sangalpa' which binds you to many things outside? Haven't you realised that if there is no *sangalpa* or consciousness, the objects outside will stay as two entities without any attachment and one will never be able to establish a bond and repeatedly fall into the pit of agony. Your attraction and desire to possess the quietness also contributes to the restlessness in you."

She went on to tell me the story of *Ghadhi* quoting Vasista sudha to explain what is *maya*, "In fact, anything we see is a reflection or projection of our own creation. We throw the seed of love, hatred, anger, etc. in us outside and they alone germinate. When we do not respond to external disturbances silence prevails in the mind, which leads to unwavering thoughts. It is only such a kind of stillness that can give you happiness or a kind of quietness that is known as *mukti*." She quoted and lectured on several matters from the Vedas and Upanishads and I remained shell shocked to hear such high philosophies from the mouth of my wife. So, the source of her calmness and composure was her knowledge. Is she the afterlife of Mythreyi or Ghargi born to teach me the basics of Veda? I had wasted my time roaming around when the treasure house was so near me. At her advice, we denounced everything and became mendicants walking the narrow streets of Madurai. One day, we escaped from the body to nature.

13

Waking up from the reverie

I gently extricated myself from the world of the past. I was still smarting with the pain of the miserable lives I had lived through when I noticed Partha sitting quietly on the sofa. He smilingly asked me whether I was alright and whether I was happy to have travelled to the past and seen the lives I had lived.

"Yes, Partha. I have seen and lived them all. But my mind is still gloating on the banks of the Saraswathy. What happened to you after my fall in the war we fought together?" I inquired inquisitively so I could learn of what had happened after my death.

"Don't you remember what I told you while familiarizing myself to you?" Partha reminded me. "I removed your body from the scene, escaping the eyes of our enemies, and rode fast into the forest. I buried your body deep within the ground with the help of some of our soldiers. The war continued for some more days and when everything was coming to an end, I was killed by a rebel's arrow when the council was discussing the future plan of action."

"Partha, I am still dazed. Am I dreaming or seeing you live? Nobody would believe this," I wondered.

"If somebody heard about my visit, they would brush it aside as a fabricated story. Within a couple of days, you will also forget what happened and believe that it was a dream or a wild imagination," Partha laughed.

"Your people are still unsure about the existence of extra-terrestrial societies and are trying to send radio signals to the nearest cosmic chums expecting a reply. But, my friend, there are a number of technologically adept societies in the cosmos, the science of those extra-terrestrial beings is far superior than those who have obsolete technologies and you will not be able to reach them. I told you earlier that our technologies are thousands of years ahead of you. There are aliens out there walking with you but you are not aware of their presence. They are more evolved and sometimes not adept to physical forms like me. I can see the prowling aliens on the earth who have come with different purposes. They have mostly travelled to earth out of scientific inquisitiveness without any malign intentions of troubling the planet or the habitants. Otherwise, your earth would have been reduced to ashes a long time ago."

"You mean to say that the way fax has replaced telex and the explosion in the digital world is changing our communication facilities? Maybe our tools are obsolete and incompatible with the advanced outfits of inhabitants out there in the Universe. However, is it true that the invocations of the sufferings on earth will be heard by the guardian Gods?" I was becoming excited by Partha's explanations.

"Well. You call 'Them' God or by any name. They are the protectors who receive the distress signals and address them suitably. However, the cosmic law forbids aliens from undertaking any task in the alien form and exercising their supernatural powers. They have to become an integral part of the particular planet to act and so, they normally take birth in that planet as one of its inhabitants, abiding their time, culture and prevailing beliefs. Nevertheless, the alien protectors born as creatures of the planet will have vestigial powers that enable them to connect to their parent society and receive help in complicated situations," Partha said.

"Well that may be the reason they are all born to virgin mothers as incarnations during different periods to destroy evil and save earth. There are incidents quoted in the epics of their sojourns to other planets to secure new powers to exercise in emergent circumstances..."

I interrupted him, "Partha, is it possible that the rogues from certain planets can similarly show up on other planets with analogous clouts?"

"Oh. Sure. Those reprobates are also capable of entering the system of a planet so that they can implement their evil designs and dominate all the fields," he agreed, "however, such an entry is possible only by corrupting the minds of the inhabitants who sport unethical lifestyles. A clean mind is beyond corruption and there comes the play of spiritualism as a means to fend the borders and deflect evil. You may remember the Yogis on the banks of Saraswathy River who were aware of the expanse of the Universe and how they preached about psychosomatic-spiritual discipline to achieve union and harmony between mind, body, and soul, finally realising the ultimate union of an individual consciousness with the Universal consciousness."

"Yes. I remember and am aware of the necessity to keep the mind clean of malicious thoughts to defend against the demonic feelings."

"Kumar, You may know that the protectors function in a timeless realm and also within time. They are virtuous extra-terrestrial beings engaged in routing those from the rogue planets who deviate from the Universal law," he further added.

"In the case of individual planets, the good-hearted lot fight those with evil minds whose activities and interests are harmful to the society and in turn to the planet itself," Partha said. The battle between Protectors and rogues is a timeless issue revolving around the security of the cosmos. The battles fought by the incarnations quoted in the Puranas and epics are a testimony to the act of the Protectors occurring in *Yuga* cycles. Any tangential advance of brainpower is unsafe to the rhythm of the Universe. The battle between the good and bad on any individual planet revolves around inappropriate social conduct and time-tested ethics that form the history of that planet. Again, characters like Rama and Krishna in your epics were born in different periods to wipe out evil to ensure the sustenance of virtues in the masses."

"But Partha, when you say the *Yuga* cycles I am still confused about the time frames because Rama was said to be born in the *Treta Yuga*, which covers a span of a million years. But as per the dating done on the Ramayana, based on astronomical information such as position of constellations and time of eclipses as given in the scriptures, Ramayana took place somewhere in 7000 BC."

"Kumar, the scenes and position of constellations repeat in their hundreds of years of orbiting. Don't you remember that in the *Ramayana* Rama wondering whether he had fought a similar war in a different *Yuga* with a faint remembrance of his earlier incarnations?"

I wondered at his thorough reading of the ancient books and epics.

"Partha, I remember the stories of the supernatural realm inhabited by an array of powerful deities who need to be placated with ceremonial offerings and ritual practices. Several cultures around the globe believe in several levels such as heaven and the underworld with mortal worlds sandwiched in between. I have heard of the rise and fall of several mediators between the mortals and the supernatural realm."

"You don't have to placate the guardians to get their favour," Partha countered. "They monitor the activities on the planets with a bigger lens than we can imagine and appear at appropriate times to set things right. It may be an intervention to protect an individual's plea or the masses. Whatever may be the purpose, your mind alone is the mediator between the protector and you. The rest is the assumption of helpless minds," Partha added.

"Are you suggesting that the protectors take birth on planets and live like the residents engaged in fights with the rogues? Do you mean like the congregations of those supporters of virtuous and malevolent on different sides engaged in wars for achieving everlasting peace?"

"Yes, something very similar. But everlasting peace is a myth. There are wars taking place on several planets. That is what I meant by the timeless and diverse issues of the cosmos and planets. This will go on and on. The departed soul or spirit from different planets will find a place on different levels of the cosmos in accordance with the virtue of their deeds and inclinations."

"Partha, I understand that part. But the one that bothers me is about changing morals, principles, etc. Over time, principles that had once appeared reasonable and virtuous become ridiculous and questionable. When I probe history, I find that notions of virtue change over time and assume different meanings in different parts of the world."

"My dear friend, haven't you read the great teacher Acharya Sankara's commentaries that dharma, which is the law of life, is relative to place, time, and circumstance," Partha snapped. "It is not a rigid procrustean bed to which every person is tied, whatever he is and wherever he is. Hence, cultures seem to be relative adjustments and envisagement or outlooks of mankind under certain geographical and social conditions. My dear Kumar, I wish you would look at justice, virtues, and philosophies from a holistic point of view. Nobody knows how things work in the Universe. Your individual gain or loss is not the ultimate aim of anything that happens in the world or the Universe. Similarly, people have justifications for all their actions. They are all individual perceptions. But when you try to unify the individual happenings with the ultimate result, you will be able to understand how the Universe works. It is like unifying the individual consciousness with the Universal consciousness to realize the Super Power or GOD as extolled in the *Bhagavad Gita*.

The underlying principle is that the beings should be able to realise the celestial potential through social behaviour. In order to understand the right and wrong of actions, we have to realise the very obvious contrast between evolved species and the rest of nature. Only such species have the ability to trim the bad laws to reap constructive results. This means we appreciate and include others in our quest for the security of the system as a whole and ensure its progress. This is the justice of time. Attachment to materials and a craving for power will prompt exploitation of others and foil the mission of achieving security and progress. This results in the decay of justice. Virtue alone ensures that we are able to subdue these cravings for power, fame, and domination."

"Oh Partha, this is what Lord Krishna delivered to Partha in the *Bhagavad Gita*. Here Partha is conveying the same to Kumar, the mortal," I laughed jokingly.

"Oh. I have come across that great character in your history. He may be an alien guardian from a supernatural realm. You should also remember his words that the energy with genetic and acquired characters escapes the body and enters a new body. Your body is not you but you are what the consciousness tells you. Your journey through the past lives must have shown you that we never die and our basic characters get transferred with opportunities to refine them," Partha reminded me of the scenes of my past lives that he had projected for me.

"Kumar, your doubt is genuine and it happens so. Apart from this you may know that the evolved species of the planets are mostly aliens from outside. Just look at the varied human framework, skin colours, food habits, the tastes for materials and the characters."

Partha was springing more surprises at me.

"You mean the inhabitants are all aliens from different planets? Don't you think diversity is the result of a genetic inheritance from our ancestors and skin colour and food habits are a result of the climatic vicissitudes?" I asked in amazement.

"Of course, it is the genetic inheritance from your ancestors who landed at different locations on earth during different times and you are all descendants of those aliens. There has been a mixing of blood and cultures through the years. But the fundamental outlook of these people differs and the fight on the earth is between descendants of aliens with contrasting interests. This is partly true on other planets too. Mortals have a complicated identity. The migration of people from place to place throughout history has exacerbated the confusion. The jobs of the protectors become tougher and it becomes increasingly difficult to identify the evil characters amongst all the people and bring them together to one battleground and bleed the evil characters altogether. There is a cosmic law that has to be abided and respected by all in the Universe. Aberrations will alter the rhythm and hence any such attempts will be thwarted by Universal guardians whether it happens in outer space or on some planet," Partha elaborated.

"Of course, it is a hard job for the protectors to identify the evil characters, coerce them to converge in a common place and ensure they are killed."

I thought about the Mahabharata war and the self-destruction of the Yadavas as had been predicted in the Vishnu Purana. During the Kurukshetra war, such a pooling of malicious characters, and their annihilation in the battlefield, was ensured by Lord Krishna. Later, the wicked ones in his own clan were wiped out in the fight that ensued between them.

On hearing my friend that humans were descendants of aliens, my mind drifted to the "Reptilian Elite" theory about which I had read. I asked Partha whether there was any truth in the belief that in ancient times a group of advanced reptiles from the Alpha Draconic star system came to Earth and infiltrated the governments of the ancient civilizations in order to control all the humans, enslave them, and became their rulers. I continued to ask him whether it was possible that they bred with other humans to form crossbreeds so that their DNA infiltrated human minds. They could control us since their DNA was inside our systems.

"Well. It is difficult to isolate one such incident in the 4. 5 billion years of life on your planet as an exclusive one. The probability of similar incidents is not unlikely," Partha quipped.

Partha's comment prompted me to think of the depictions of the ancient Egyptian God, Anubis, with the head of a jackal and Narasimha with the lion's head, monkey faced gods, etc., in Hindu mythology. However, there had not been a mixing of their genes with humans. Alternatively, snakes have been historically worshiped in several countries, and continue to be worshipped in several places. There are several references. But do they only reflect cultural migration over a period of time? Several things skimmed through my mind while talking to Partha.

"So, may I take that the wonderful sculptures in many temples, which are thousands of years old, around the globe with figurines of animals and men could be the handiwork of aliens and those artefacts could be facsimiles of the habitants of other world?" I hopped from the subject of beliefs to unexplained architectural wonders that were an impossible feat for humans with undeveloped technologies in ancient times.

"I told you earlier that some aliens who were born on earth had vestigial powers so they could establish links with their parent planets or neighbouring planets, and these could be the work of those aliens who were capable of travelling back and forth in time. They could also be designs of time travellers who are yet to be born on earth as a result of genetic mutation," Partha added.

"You have several questions for me, my friend, but you have answers to them that can be retrieved from within through absolute concentration. This is the experience of the great sages who were born on your planet and mine. When thoughts and words reach a point, and find no way beyond, it is the absolute understanding of the Universe."

"I am sorry, dear. It is time I join my colleagues on the return journey to our planet," Partha gave me a jolt. "I am happy about this unexpected meeting. We can never say when we will meet again because the permutation combination of matter in the Universe is a mystery. You may be born on our planet or I may be pushed back to earth when my time expires on my planet," Partha said with an expression of helplessness.

The sudden notice of his departure was a shock for me. I didn't know how to respond and cried in exasperation at the thought of missing him forever. "When will we meet again?" I asked him in desperation. "Oh! Partha, I may miss you forever. I don't expect to meet you again during my lifetime," I nearly cried in anxiety.

"My dear friend," Partha continued "time is a measurable period that lacks spatial dimensions and your time is irrelevant to other species in the cosmos. You might remember the character 'Leela' whom you mentioned earlier. If you are blessed, an alien or as you said the deity you worship may land you on my planet. But nothing lasts forever in the Universe. The scenes keep changing but there will be remote connections between things that keep us wondering whether anything was ever real. Don't you remember what we were taught in the Gurukul along the banks of Saraswathy? The creatures of the planets cannot visualise the shore they will reach after disappearance from the mortal world since the future is the result of the past and present. Those who can foresee will never divulge their secrets. That is the natural law of the cosmos."

"I understand what you are saying. I am convinced about it after seeing and hearing you Partha," I admitted.

He came to me and embraced me. Suddenly, he disappeared without notice, leaving me aghast. We were in the middle of a conversation and he left all of a sudden as if he did not want to prolong the dialogue.

14

Return to Reality

"Why are you sitting and sleeping on the sofa?" my wife jolted me to the real world. I just could not make out whether I had been sleeping or daydreaming.

"Hay..." I started to say something to my wife who was pulling me back to the bedroom. Before I could spill some words, she was already cuddled in bed ready to go back to sleep.

"I thought you had gone to the bathroom. I waited for some time and when you did not return, I went to the hall to look for you. What happened?" She asked me out of concern with closed eyes.

I didn't want to spoil her sleep, so I said, "Nothing, dear. I got up suddenly and couldn't go back to sleep, so I thought about sitting on the sofa for a while."

"Ok," she said. The next minute, she was snoring gently.

Well, I thought. My wife was clocking my disappearance from the bedroom for a few minutes. However, we were both unsure about when I left the bed. The gap couldn't be much but in that lapse of time the meeting with my extra-terrestrial friend had occurred. I had travelled thousands of years backward in time with his help and seen five of my earlier lives. I had also been engaged in a long conversation with my friend. I could not dismiss what had been experienced as an illusion. It was all real for me. But as my friend had warned me, nobody would believe me and I would be a laughing stock in front of others if I tried to speak about the meeting.

Dreams normally last for a few seconds, but one can feel as if they have been dreaming throughout the night. I just couldn't make out in which stage of sleep I had entertained the visit of my friend.

The Mandukya Upanishad describes four states of consciousness, namely waking (jagrat), dreaming (svapna), and deep sleep (suṣhupti), which correspond to the Three Bodies Doctrine in Hinduism. They are often equated with the five Koshas (sheaths), which cover the 'Atman'. Had I been in the waking stage when we are aware of our daily world, i. e. outward knowing which the gross body is. I am not sure. The second is the dreaming mind detailed as inward knowing subtle and burning subtle body. But it had not been a dream since I was aware of the surroundings. The third state is deep sleep, a state in which the underlying ground of consciousness is distracted and you partly merge with the inner controller or Atman. My consciousness was definitely preoccupied. The fourth factor is *Turiya*, the pure consciousness which is the background that underlies and transcends the three common states of consciousness where the dualistic experience is no longer felt. I was not part of the dualistic state since I was conscious of myself and my surroundings. I was in a phase in which space and time were unconnected as if in deep sleep but consciousness truncated through the dream stage to the waking state.

My experience under such conditions couldn't be considered either a delusion or similar to the illusion Narada experienced. Narada was a god-sage, famous in Hindu tradition, who was a travelling musician and storyteller. He transmitted news and enlightening wisdom. He was one of the mind created children of Brahma. He was presented as a sage with absolute devotion to Lord Vishnu. Though 'He' was gifted with the boon of knowledge of knowing past, present, and future, the knowledge of *Maya* eluded him. He got a flavour of *Maya* the minute Lord Krishna was asked about it. The Lord asked him to fetch a glass of water since he was parched because they were sitting on a river bank under the hot sun. Narada walked to a nearby village to fetch potable water. There, he saw a beautiful woman at the doorstep of one of the huts. Narada immediately fell for her and asked for her hand in marriage. They were soon married and he fathered several children. He lived a long life with her, but one day a great flood engulfed their village and Narada called out for the help of Lord Krishna in distress. Once he forgot the world and sought the feet of the Lord, he immediately got out of the trance and realised that he was sitting on the same rock on which he had been sitting with the Lord before he had posed the question of *Maya* to the Lord. The Lord clarified that what happened to him or was experienced by him in the reverie was *Maya*. Thus, even though *Maya* though connotes a 'magic show, an illusion where things appear to be present but are not what they seem', the spiritual concept implies 'that which exists, but is constantly changing and thus is spiritually unreal'.

However, I am unable to jest what I had experienced as a dream, *Maya*, illusion, or hallucination. I was in a confused stage like the perplexity misted phase of Leela's husband in 'Leelopakyanam', one of the stories told by Vasista in 'Vasista sudha' to a totally depressed Sri Rama when he saw the worldly miseries. Vasista illustrates many examples of the transient nature of the matters in the world to Sri Rama. Leelopakyanam is one of the stories narrated to demonstrate the deceptive or illusory nature of life. Whether we are actually living or dreaming a life according to our *Vasanas*, i. e. the inherent qualities are a puzzle. In 'Leelopakyanam' in the concluding chapter when Leela's husband was about to consider everything he had seen about his previous lives as a dream, the meeting with the Brahmins who were returning after observing the 'Chandrayana Vratha' flabbergasted him since he was unable to figure out whether the flashes of his past lives were delusions or reality.

I was unable to sleep. My mind was screaming with the flow of hundreds of thoughts. The first and foremost thought was that most of Partha's observations were nothing new. They were all enshrined in Hindu, Greek, and Maya philosophies about which I had read. Life never ends as such but continues carrying the basic characters, and when you are reborn you have umpteen chances to refine yourself. The scenes of my past life and the conversation with my alien friend kept appearing in front of me. I tried to make my own assessment about how much I had refined myself throughout the previous births I had so far endured or enjoyed.

It was very obvious that there was an invisible connection between my lives from my birth on the banks of 'Saraswathy River' to the current one. What I was before my birth as a Partha's friend still eludes me. My character has changed but not significantly. I am still the same confused man but over several births I have attained some kind of control over my mind. It also seemed as if the same woman had been reborn as my partner in all the births and remained like a hope in crisis.. Whenever I sank in the deep waters of distress, she had resuscitated me back to life. A fish doesn't know water until it escapes the hands of the fisherman and returns to the water. Similarly, whenever I struggled in the waters of *samsara sagara* some force pulled me back to the shore. In spite of the lessons I had learnt about the unworthiness of life and its transient nature, the weight of the tendencies in me (call them the *prarabdha*, burden or bundle of cravings) would slide me back into the *Samasara koopa* (worldly pool of miseries).

I am reminded of the story of Vritrasura, a demon by birth but an exalted *bhakti yogi* in mind who was able to propound deep transcendental knowledge even in the midst of a fight with Indra, the king of the heavens. Vritrasura prompted Indra to keep fighting but never stopped the philosophical discourses. He was sure about his end, which he considered a blissful extermination from the slush of demonic life. Indra wondered how a yogi like him could have fallen from the path of righteousness and gone uncanny. Vritrasura smilingly conveyed that in spite of his spiritual advancement, the genetic inheritance of the *rakshasa* qualities had prevented him from staying virtuous. Though I am no comparison to such noble characters, I feel that my genetic legacy may be a reason for my failure to realise absolute truth.

'When we talk about genetic inheritance or karma vasana you are pulling something along with you from time unknown without an idea of its influence on you'. My mind went back again to the conversation with Partha.

"Partha, do you mean that preordained decrees are the result of actions emanating from desires embedded in you which is the *karma vasana*?"

Partha didn't immediately answer but smiled and gestured to me to continue.

"You have no help with *vasanas*. You have to perform them since you are already set in motion like an arrow shot from a bow that you can't take it back."

"When the lives you lived so far were unreeled you would have seen how the inherent qualities followed you through all your births in one form or another, but Kumar you had chances to amend your character in every life you lived just like creating new computer programmes that are friendly. This is what you had carried forward to simulate in the new body with a less undesirable impact on nature. So, you were becoming eco-friendly slowly," Partha mused.

"May I remind you about the articles you read on computer simulation that can explain this further scientifically?" Partha continued. "You may know that you are the brain computer simulations of the 'Super brain' from which the sensory data is transmitted. You respond to the transmitted message because your brain is captivated by the connection and you start acting as per the transferred information. The super brain may be acting and interacting with the simulated world and getting feedback. You, the simulation, may be induced by any number of possible means to recall temporarily or otherwise that you are inside a virtual realm like the passage of a soul from an earthly body to an afterlife. That may be why the oldies sometimes call us avatar, which manifests itself differently but is the true consciousness of the Super brain. So, you are living in a simulated reality of a real one. And so, believe there is truth in seeing the world and the entities as *Maya*. Now, you would want to know about the reference world. Humans or extra-terrestrial beings like me cannot say with absolute sceptical certainty that we are experiencing reality or a virtual simulation since we too are well within a simulated world. Perhaps the so-called supernatural beings do not have real bodies either in the external reality of the physical world, because they could also be simulated entities who possess an appropriate level of consciousness that is implemented using the simulation's own logic. It is also possible that a simulated entity could be taken out of the simulation entirely by means of a mind transfer into a synthetic body."

"As you must have read," Partha dissected the theory further to explain how the individual functions, "it could be that you, the earthly being, as well the extra-terrestrials could be a system of intelligence that perceives its environment and takes advantageous actions to ensure its chances of success but may sometimes land in failures as well."

"The simulations may be inculcated intelligence or artificial intelligence with possibilities to create and solve problems using built in devices with techniques from probability theory. Ultimately, a programme is created which works out in a fashion designed by you," Partha concluded.

"Partha," I intervened out of excitement, "Is it that any programme that is developed by an individual may have some connection to the embedded information and the imprints of the tendencies in it and any intent and action influences the future?"

"Kumar, this resembles the karmic theory held by Hinduism, Buddhism, Jainism, Christianity, Judaism and Sikhism. Good intent and good deed (deed or intent that does not interfere with natural law) will contribute to good karma and future happiness. While the other leads to bad future suffering. So, it is the perception—the ability to use input from the sensors to deduce aspects of the world. All in all, the Super head simulated brain is me and I am the supreme head, i. e. there is no duality and there is only a Universal self and anything else is its reflection. You have several programmes and functions in the computer module. Which programme you choose depends on your inclination or interest. Simulations choose the compatible programme that will lead to discovering its attachment with the main computer. Once you get linked with a super computer there is a flood into which you fall and you are unable to realize the duality. This is the merger of you with the Universe advocated in the *Vedas*, *Upanishads*, and *Bhagavad Gita*.

"That is an amalgamation of science and belief, Partha."

"Further, you may look into evolutionary theory in this regard and its connection to the simulated brain that your scientists have explained. You may see that individuals are generally programmed to behave in ways that ensure survival," Partha concluded.

15

Recapitulation

I was a good friend of Partha when I was born in Dholavira village on the banks of Saraswathy but had unknowingly sported a kind of envy unknown to me towards his success and recognition among the public. In spite of the spiritual lessons I had taken my mind remained in turmoil. On the one hand, the suppressed desires suffocated me and on the other hand, the knowledge about the wasteful nature of material benefits doused the lusts flaming in me whenever I made an advancement to achieve them. I loved power and money which were considered our worst enemies by the village elders. My oscillating and vacillating mind made me wretched always and I spent most of my time trying to overcome my bitterness with overconfidence and over zealousness inviting trouble most of the time. My wife and Partha were aware of the aberrations in me but ignored them and bailed me out of danger on several occasions acknowledging the all loving and helpful nature in me and the great skills I possessed on many fronts. However, instead of appreciating their help, it would hurt my ego and confound my already tormented emotions. In such frenzy, I had ignored Partha's warnings and gone into the midst of the enemies and ended myself.

I had carried all those cravings, as well as my wavering mind, with me to the next life. I was born to a king and inherited the kingdom to rule as I wished in the last life. I had power in my hand but failed miserably to execute my duties because my mind kept oscillating between art and administration. When I was stripped of my power by the enemy, instead of fighting back I tried to escape behind the curtain of spiritualism. It seemed as if the same rustic lady who had tried to steer me to the right path in my previous life had been born as my queen to revitalise me and regain the lost power. Finally, I skidded on to the path of redemption because of her.

My next birth as a gold explorer in the Aravalli in Rajasthan has a remote connection to my current life in terms of the job pursued as well as the spiritualistic inclinations. Except for this similarity and the passion for pilgrimages, the other inherent demonic characteristics apparent in me in the former lives appeared subdued in the worker in the Aravalli. My partner was an impressive devotee of Krishna who charmed me, the Aravalli explorer, by her innocence and dedication to the cause of all fellow beings. Her loss drove me nuts and finally to death while wandering the streets of Haridwar.

It was intriguing for me that I had been born as an animal in the fourth birth. Perhaps, the aggregated animal instincts and the craziness for power in me manifested itself in the form of a lion. I had all the time in the world to meditate and achieve new heights in thinking but being an animal, the waves of thoughts had limited reach which depressed and frustrated me to such an extent that I finally sought solace in the deep waters of the river. There too the lady made an appearance as my queen but left me after some time, probably out of despair at her incapacity to help my anguish or her own.

The confused man in the prior births torn between attachments and detachments emerged as yet another chaotic character in Madurai. However, that soul roamed the city and shores of different countries without the perception of the emptiness of life until the lady who had followed me in other lives materialised again as my wife, philosopher, and guide. She waited for an appropriate time, punctured my self-image, and drained out the muddled passions in me. Her poignant words exposed the naked truth about life and its unworthiness that changed the man in me.

Time rolled and I have been born again and it seems that some unburned longings still remain in me. However, when I picturise my previous births and compare the eccentricities, the bane that had shadowed me, I feel that it has lost its clutches on me. It appears that I have gained a sort of control over my mind and the rising frustrations mend easily like the ruptures in self-sealing tyres. The reluctance to feel sad or the conscious win over anger is some of the fine-tuning that has occurred in me. I try to find a way to get over ill feelings and stay sane all the time. The only accursed relic in me is the fleeting interest in many different matters. During my school days, I had developed a liking for painting and pencil sketching apart from lessons. The fondness for them faded with time and then during my college days, I was eager to write short stories, none of which were printed. That didn't depress me and decided to follow the advice of publishers to continue the pursuit of writing. Unfortunately, my interest in writing also slowly waned with time. The only interest that has persisted since my college days is philosophy and the yearning to understand the much talked about 'knowledge' or 'absolute truth'. *Upanishads, Srimad Bhagavatham, Bhagavad Gita, Bible*, or any philosophic treatises attracted me and kept me engaged. But the botch is that the philosophies would vaporise during times of distress and I would not be able to recall anything. However, I would soon hark for the same philosophies I had temporarily deserted as a remedy to stabilise the mind. This swing and fight in my mind goes on and on, probably helping the decontamination of the thoughts. In the process, the apparent sophistication I have gained so far is that situations don't perturb me that easily and love or hatred has lost meaning for me. Riches or fame neither excite nor does their loss dampen my spirit and such consciousness helps to keep the miseries at bay.

Every person has distinct bad and good character in them and depending on the dominance of either one an individual is branded as a good or bad soul. Most cultures in the world believe in good and bad souls and advise you to develop the good character in you to win over the bad instincts.

We all keep swirling in the material world and live in our thoughts. Our thoughts and resultant actions frame us as good or bad people. We don't need the intervention of rishis to churn the virtues out of us like they did on Vena, the evil king. A voodooist is not required to split the soul to save our good self either. We can define ourselves by self-realising the dwarf, the symbol of evil, and *Prithu*, the embodiment of virtue in us.

I think the same petite lady of few words, fully entrenched in 'bhakti', has been born again and is sharing my thoughts and feelings with me. She used to quote J. Krishnamoorthy, "If you begin to understand what you are without trying to change it, then what you undergo is a transformation."

When the events in the bygone days were screened in my mind, irrespective of whether they were pleasant or utterly disappointing, I understood that I had never been happy or jubilant whenever the desired matter landed in my lap or totally upset when it had eluded my grasp. I am consciously aware of the aspirations that stem out of *ahamgara*, i. e. the desire to stand out in everything or to show off that you are better than others. The moment that aspiration to become something sparks I am no longer free. Ambitions go haywire and thoughts jump from one branch to another, and attempts to secure the targeted matter make me restless and mad. This restlessness has enhanced the level of sleepless nights hurting my body and mind. Had I been in such a state of restlessness when I encountered my friend, Partha?

After pondering over the acts in my past lives and the life I live now, I have a feeling that the so-called successes or failures have all been illusions. The closer I was to something the greater had been the worry whether it had been for material benefit or entertaining a human relationship. When the material eludes, the lost feeling lasts until a new desire pops up.

Though I have recognized the fruitlessness of the activities in my births, I have not fully succeeded in detaching myself while performing an act. However, I feel I have matured to the extent of bravely recognising my failures openly. Is such a realization without an iota of change in the basic character called transformation or metamorphism? Is it the path we must take for the acquirement of the much talked about "knowledge' in the Upanishads?

Certainly, how can you learn what is right without knowing what was wrong? Similarly, without seeing the par excellence of things how can you conclude that it was the best and most ideal? Brahma after creating the worlds did not know how he could alleviate the sufferings of the creations. From his heart throb was born Vasista, the 'suddhabrahmam'. However, Brahma cursed his son to undergo the sufferings of the world and after a dream-like endurance of the same, Vasista asked Brahma why he had been cursed, what was the reason for the sufferings of beings, and how it could be alleviated. Brahma smiled and told him that he was cursed because he wanted him to experience the world and then ask questions. Brahma gave 'brahmopadesam' to his son and ordered him to stay with the people on earth and counsel them about the truth. It looks like there could be only one truth and that would emerge from churning the untrue, unworthy life. Partha had given me a chance to get a glimpse of the travels my soul/energy had made so far. All the births had been in tune with the inherent qualities. However, in all the lives there had been chances to shed the filth and cleanse myself. I wonder how many lives I may have to live further to realise the 'absolute truth' that has escaped my comprehension.

The Nadi astrologer in the precinct of Vaitheeswaran temple told me about my previous birth and that of my wife in Madurai as screened to me by Partha. However, I am sceptical about his prediction that this will be our last life on earth since I feel I have not acquired the 'knowledge' so far. Is the realisation of the fact that the 'knowledge' is still far from me the 'Absolute truth' that will unify me with the Universal self?

"Your reality is a holographic simulation. We are a fragment of the 'Absolute' expressing ourselves within a cosmic video game. Theoretically, human consciousness may continue to expand the horizons of its perceptual capability until it reaches the dimension of the Absolute at which point perception stops because the Absolute generates no holograms of or about itself," Partha's words still rang in my ears.

As quantum physics has shown and what science recently confirms, there is no such thing as matter. Everything is light vibrating at specific frequencies. Humans can only perceive less than 1% of the light and audio spectrum. Suddenly, the paranormal, transcendental, and spiritual, as well as the paradoxical sayings of the mystics throughout the ages all make sense.

That may be what the ancients meant by achieving enlightenment: to transcend out of the simulation into the Absolute.

What is that knowledge? 'Knowledge' is the state of realisation in which one sees himself in all beings and all beings in him. Bliss is the very nature of the self, the Supreme State. It is devoid of birth, existence, destruction, recognition and experience.

"The secret of life is to 'die before you die'
and find that there is no death."

Eckhart Tolle

Glossary

Acharya Sankara – Adi Shankaracharya was an Indian philosopher who consolidated the doctrine of Advaita Vedanta.

Aapasthamba Sutra – One of the oldest Dharma related Sanskrit texts of Hinduism.

Anityam – Impermanent.

Arjuna. – Arjuna is the main protagonist of the Indian epic *Mahabharata* and also appears in other ancient Hindu texts including the *Bhagavata Purana*. In the epic, he is the third among the Pandavas, the five sons of Pandu.

Asura – An adjective meaning "powerful" or "mighty" which in Indian mythology tends to be evil

Avanti – An ancient Indian kingdom in the territory of Madhya Pradesh.

Atman – A person's soul/ considered as immanent in an individual's real self.

Bhakti – Personal worship of God.

Brihadeeswara temple –An ancient shrine situated in Thanjavur, Tamil Nadu

Brahma – Creator God in Hinduism.

Bhakti yogi – Is one engaged in spiritual practice within Hinduism focused on loving devotion towards any personal deity.

Brahmopadesom – The Supreme Teaching of Lord Brahma.

Bhagavath Gita - A Hindu Scripture comprising of 700 verses that is part of epic *Mahabharata*

Bhadrinad – A holy town and a Nagar panchayat in Chamoli district in the state of Uttarakhand, India

Chandrayana vritha – One of the ancient, traditional forms of Fasting (Upavasana) sometimes done as part of a punishment and atonement for certain offences and transgressions.

Chedi kingdom – An ancient Indian mahajanapada, a Kingdom which fell roughly in the Bundelkhand division of Madhya Pradesh

Chera King – One of the principal lineages in the early history of the present-day states of Kerala and Tamil Nadu in southern India

Chikitsak – Physician

Chola emperor – A tamil thalassocratic empire of southern India,

Chudamani Vihara – A Buddhist vihara (monastery) in Nagapattinam, Tamil Nadu.

Computer simulation – It is the process of mathematical modelling, performed on a computer, which is designed to predict the behaviour or outcome of a real-world or physical system.

Dharma – Code of life.

Dholavira – An archaeological site at Khadirbet in Bhachau Taluka of Kutch District, in the state of Gujarat in western India

Dharsan – Darśana is the auspicious sight of a deity or a holy person.

Devas – A class of divine beings in the Vedic period, which in Indian religion are benevolent.

Duryodhana – A major character in the *Mahabharata*, the eldest of the Kauravas.

Ganesh – One of the best-known and most worshipped deities in the Hindu Pantheon.

Gargi – An ancient Indian philosopher in Vedic literature

Gopis – referred to as "cowherd girls," according to the esoteric theology of Vaishnavism

Gir Forest – Wildlife Sanctuary near Talala *Gir* in Gujarat, India

Gurukul – A gurukul or gurukulam is a type of education system in ancient India with shishya, the pupil, living near or with the guru in the same house.

Jara – The hunter who was the instrument for Lord Krishna's departure from the world.

Jalasamadhi – Freeing one's self from the troubles of life by drowning

Janma – In simplest terms, it means Birth.

Janmashtami – An annual Hindu festival that celebrates the birth of Krishna, the eighth incarnation of Vishnu.

Jeevatma – In simplest terms, Jeevatma is a term given for an individual soul

Karmic theory – A karma theory considers the action and intentions to be the causative factor for the results and the concept thus encourages each person to seek and live a moral life.

Krishna – A major deity in Hinduism. He is worshipped as the eighth avatar of Vishnu and also as the supreme God in his own right.

Kjani – Knowledgeable person

Kannayya – One of many childhood names of Lord Krishna

Karna – One of the major characters of the *Mahabharata*.

Kosa – kosa is a unit of measurement in ancient India and is about 3000 meters or 1. 8 miles

Kurushetra war – A war described in the *Mahabharata*

Loka – In the cosmography of Hinduism, the universe or any particular division of it.

Leela – One of the characters in 'Leelopakyanam' in Vasista Sudha

Mathura – Mathura is a sacred city in Uttar Pradesh, northern India where the deity Lord Krishna is said to have been born.

Maya – Illusion

Matsya Kingdom – Matsya Kingdom was one of the solasa Mahajanapadas during Vedic era as described in the *Mahabharata.*

Manusmriti – An ancient legal text and constitution among the many Dharmaśāstras of Hinduism.

Mahabharatha – One of the two major Sanskrit epics of ancient India,

Mukti – In Indian philosophy and religion, liberation from the cycle of death and rebirth

Mythreyi – One of the most learned and virtuous women of ancient India

Nadi jyosian – Nadi josiyam is a form of Dharma astrology practiced in Tamil Nadu, India and adjacent regions in India. It is based on the belief that the past, present, and future lives of all humans were foreseen by Dharma sages in ancient times. Nadi astrology uses a sidereal zodiac system.

Nithyam – Always, constantly, regularly.

Narasimha – A fierce incarnation of the Hindu god Vishnu in the form of part lion and part man to destroy evil and end religious persecution.

Pandya Kingdom – A dynasty of south India, one of the three famous Tamil lineages

Paramatma – The Supreme soul.

Pandits – A Hindu scholar learned in Sanskrit and Hindu philosophy and religion, typically also a practising priest.

Parasurama – The sixth incarnation of Vishnu in Hinduism

Pakkanar – A character in Malayalam Folklore

Pandu Putras – Refers to the five brothers namely, Yudhishthira (Or Dharma), Bhima, Arjuna, Nakula and Sahadeva, who are the main characters in the epic Mahabharata.

Puranas – Ancient and old and it is a vast genre of Indian literature about a wide range of topics, particularly legends and other traditional lore. It discusses a wide range of topics including cosmology, astronomy, genealogy, geography, legend, music, dance, yoga and culture

Prithu – Celebrated as the first consecrated king, from whom the earth received her (Sanskrit) name Prithvi.

Ramayana – Rāmāyana is one of the two major Sanskrit epics of ancient India.

Rukmani – A Hindu goddess and the chief consort of Krishna, the king of Dvaraka.

Rishikesh – Rishikesh is a city in India's northern state of Uttarakhand, in the Himalayan foothills beside the Ganges River

Rishis – A Hindu sage or saint.

Sanjayan – A character from the Mahābhārata.

Sanadhana Dharma – Denote the "eternal" or absolute set of duties or religiously ordained practices incumbent upon all Hindus, regardless of class, caste, or sect.

Sanyasam-Monasticism

Sourashtra – Some part of it also known as Sorath or Kathiawar, is a peninsular region of Gujarat, India.

Sadhu – A religious ascetic, mendicant or any holy person in Hinduism and Jainism who has renounced the worldly life.

Slokas – A couplet of Sanskrit verse.

Simhala – Refers to the successive Sinhalese kingdoms that existed in what is today Sri Lanka.

Saivism – One of the major traditions within Hinduism that worships Lord Shiva

Sangalpa – An intention formed by the heart and mind

Srimad Bhagavata Purana – It is one of Hinduism's eighteen great Puranas.

Surya Siddhanta – A text on astronomy and time keeping

Taittiriya Upanishad – A Vedic era Sanskrit text.

Theerta – A Sanskrit word that means "crossing place, ford", and refers to any place, text or person that is holy. It particularly refers to pilgrimage sites and holy places in Hinduism as well as Jainism.

Thandavam-A divine dance

Treta yuga – The second of the four yugas, or ages of mankind, in the religion of Hinduism.

Vasana – Inherent quality

Vaikunda – Celestial abode (dwelling) of Vishnu who is the principal deity of the Universes

Vasista Sudha – Spiritual book

Varnasramam – Refers to Varnashrama-dharma – duties performed according to the system of four varnas

Vedanta – Hindu philosophy based on the doctrine of the Upanishads, especially in its monistic form.

Vedavyasa – A rishi (sage) who classified the Vedas.

Vishnu –One of the principal deities of Hinduism.

Vajranabha – Great grandson of Lord Krishna.

Vrindavan – Holy town in Uttar Pradesh, northern India. The Hindu deity Krishna is said to have spent his childhood here.

Vihara – Space or facilities for dwellings

Vritrasura – Demon king mentioned in Srimad Bhagavatam.

Vena – An evil king mentioned in Bhagavatam.

Yuga – A yuga (Sanskrit), in Hinduism, is a large period of time as it relates to the past, present and future.

Yadavas – A descendant of Yadu, who is a mythological king.

Yogi – Yogi is a practitioner of Yoga, including a sanyasin or practitioner of meditation in Indian religions.

References

Astronomical dating of Ramayana – Dr. P. V. Vartak.

"Are you living in a computer simulation"? - Nick Bostrom

Biocentrism: How Life and Consciousness are the Keys to Understanding the true Nature of the Universe. – Bob Berman and Robert Lanza.

Concepts of Reality in Hinduism and Bhuddism from the perspective of a Physicist - Kashyap Vasavada.

https://www, cpp edu>Jet 30>Vasavada 15-26

Life span: Why We Age - and Why We Don't Have to by David A Sinclair with Matthew D La Plante.

Simulation Hypothesis – Quotes from Wikipedia.

Reptilian Conspiracy theory-Wikipedia. http://content. time. com>article

Simulating Evolution - How close do computer models come to reality- Christoph Adami. May 5 2016. https://the conversation. com>Simulating-evolution-how:

Swami Krishnananda's - Divine Life Society e-books.

Speeches of J. Krishnamoorthi, philosopher, speaker and writer.

The first Modern Humans came from What is now Botswana: Study- Kerry Grens: https://www. the-scientist. com>t..

What is Silmulation theory? Are we living computer— April 1, 2021- Mike Thomas. http:builtin. com>hardware>simulation theory.

Vasista Sudha- A Hindu philosophical and spiritual text attributed to sage Valmiki.